The Quantum Mirage

Hiren Rathod

Ukiyoto Publishing

All global publishing rights are held by

Ukiyoto Publishing

Published in 2023

Content Copyright © Hiren Rathod
ISBN 9789360162139

www.ukiyoto.com

Dedicated

My Parents, My Mother Smt Dharmishthaben Kanaiyalal Rathod and Father Shree Kanaiyalal Maganlal Rathod & Special Thanks To My Sister Dr.Gopi Rathod Mavadiya.

Acknowledgments:

I would like to express my heartfelt gratitude to everyone who contributed to the creation and publication of "The Quantum Mirage." Without their support, this book would not have been possible.

First and foremost, I want to thank my family for their unwavering encouragement and belief in me. Your love and support have been my constant inspiration throughout this journey.

I extend my sincere appreciation to my editor for their invaluable insights and meticulous attention to detail. Your feedback and suggestions have significantly enhanced the quality of this manuscript.

I am indebted to my beta readers and critique partners for their honest feedback and constructive criticism. Your perspectives have helped me refine my ideas and shape this story into its final form.

I would also like to thank the professionals involved in the design and production of this book, including the cover designer and typesetter. Your creativity and talent have beautifully complemented the narrative.

To my friends, thank you for your encouragement, support, and late-night brainstorming sessions. Your camaraderie has made this writing journey all the more rewarding.

Last but not least, I want to express my deepest gratitude to the readers. Your interest in "The Quantum Mirage" and your willingness to embark on this adventure mean the world to me. I hope this book sparks your imagination and leaves you with a sense of wonder.

Thank you, one and all, for being a part of this incredible journey. Your belief in me and my work has been an immense source of motivation. May our paths continue to intertwine as we explore the boundless realms of storytelling together.

With heartfelt appreciation,

Hiren Rathod

Contents

Prologue

The Quantum Mirage is a culmination of my deep fascination with the realms of science, spirituality, and the mysteries of the universe. As a student of Computer Engineering, I have always been drawn to the vastness of the cosmos and the intricate workings of quantum physics. The idea of parallel dimensions and the concept of a multiverse have captured my imagination, inspiring me to explore the possibilities of an interconnected existence.

In this book, I sought to weave together elements of science, spirituality, and mythology, drawing from ancient wisdom and modern scientific advancements. The story follows the journey of Dr. Maya Jones and her team as they embark on a quest that blurs the boundaries between reality and imagination. Through their experiences, I aimed to delve into profound themes of self-discovery, the balance between light and dark, and the interconnectedness of all things.

While The Quantum Mirage is a work of fiction, it is my hope that readers will find within its pages a sense of wonder, inspiration, and a renewed curiosity about the mysteries that lie beyond our everyday perception. It is my belief that by exploring the realms of the unknown, we can unlock the infinite potential within ourselves and deepen our understanding of the universe.

I invite you to join Dr. Maya Jones and her team as they venture into parallel dimensions, encounter mythological creatures, and grapple with cosmic forces. Through their extraordinary journey, may you find your own path of self-discovery and embark on a quest for cosmic harmony.

Hiren Rathod

The Enigmatic Discovery

Dr. Maya Jones had always been a curious soul. As a brilliant physicist hailing from London, she had spent her life unraveling the mysteries of the universe through science and logic. But there was a longing in her heart, a yearning to explore the realms beyond what could be measured and calculated. This desire led her to make a life-altering decision—she would travel to India, the land of spirituality and ancient wisdom, to embark on a journey of self-discovery and cosmic exploration.

Arriving in Mumbai, Dr. Jones found herself immersed in the bustling energy of the city. She joined the Institute of Quantum Physics, a renowned institution at the forefront of scientific research. It was here, amidst the labyrinthine corridors and buzzing laboratories, that she stumbled upon something that would forever change the course of her life—an anomaly suggesting the existence of parallel dimensions.

Late one night, as Dr. Jones poured over the data collected from an experiment, her eyes widened in disbelief. There it was, a blip in the quantum field that defied explanation. It hinted at the existence of unseen worlds coexisting alongside our own, hidden from the gaze of ordinary perception. Excitement surged through her veins as she realized the potential implications of this discovery. The scientific community had long speculated about the existence of parallel dimensions, but evidence had always eluded them. Dr. Jones had stumbled upon something truly groundbreaking.

Determined to explore this enigma further, Dr. Jones gathered her research and prepared a presentation for her colleagues at the Institute. The following week, she stood before a room filled with physicists, computer scientists, and experts in quantum mechanics, including Dr. Asvika Bansal and Dr. Arjav Upmanyu. Nervously, yet with unwavering conviction, she began her presentation.

I have discovered something extraordinary, Dr. Jones announced, her voice filled with a mix of excitement and trepidation. Our experiments have revealed a disturbance in the quantum field that suggests the presence of parallel dimensions.

Curiosity ignited in the eyes of her colleagues as she delved into the details, explaining the anomalies observed and the potential implications for our understanding of the universe. The room buzzed with speculation and wonder. Dr. Bansal, a computer scientist known for her expertise in computational simulations, raised her hand.

Maya, have you considered developing a device that can bridge the gap between our world and these parallel dimensions? she asked, her voice tinged with excitement.

Dr. Jones nodded, her mind already racing with possibilities. That's precisely what I had in mind, she replied. We could merge cutting-edge technology with ancient Indian mantras and yantras, harnessing both science and spirituality to unlock the secrets of parallel dimensions.

Dr. Upmanyu, an expert in quantum mechanics, leaned forward, his eyes gleaming with anticipation. Imagine the doors that could open, he said. We could explore realms inspired by Indian mythology, encounter celestial beings, and uncover the remnants of ancient civilizations.

Inspired by the collaborative energy in the room, Dr. Jones and her colleagues set out on a new journey—a quest to develop a device unlike anything the world had seen before. They named it Anantakiran, a Sanskrit word meaning infinite rays. Anantakiran would be their gateway to the uncharted territories of parallel dimensions, a tool that merged technology and spirituality in a profound way.

Days turned into weeks, and weeks into months as Dr. Jones and her team poured their passion, knowledge, and expertise into the development of Anantakiran. They meticulously designed intricate circuits, encoded ancient mantras into its core, and embedded sacred yantras into its structure. It was a fusion of modern science and ancient wisdom, a testament to the harmonious coexistence of seemingly disparate realms.

Finally, after countless hours of dedication and unwavering commitment, Anantakiran was complete.

The team gathered around the device, its sleek surface shimmering with potential. They knew that their creation held the key to unveiling the mysteries of parallel dimensions.

With a mixture of anticipation and trepidation, Dr. Jones placed her hand on Anantakiran and activated its intricate mechanisms. The room filled with a soft hum as the device came to life, its screen illuminating with a brilliant array of colors and symbols. Dr. Jones and her team exchanged glances, their hearts pounding in synchrony. This was the moment they had all been waiting for—the moment when they would take their first steps into the unknown.

As they prepared to embark on their journey, the air crackled with a palpable sense of anticipation. Dr. Jones knew that the path ahead would be filled with wonders, challenges, and revelations beyond their wildest imagination. With a deep breath, she looked at her team and whispered, Let us step into the uncharted realms and uncover the secrets of the parallel dimensions.

And so, Dr. Maya Jones, Dr. Asvika Bansal, Dr. Arjav Upmanyu, and their team stepped forward, ready to venture into a realm where science and spirituality converged—a realm of infinite possibilities, awaiting their discovery.

As the team stood on the precipice of the unknown, a surge of anticipation coursed through their veins. Dr. Jones activated Anantakiran, and a pulsating energy enveloped them, transporting them beyond the boundaries of their familiar reality.

With a rush of sensations, they found themselves in a parallel dimension unlike anything they had ever experienced. The air crackled with a mystical energy, and hues of vibrant colors painted the sky. They stood in a landscape that seemed to blend elements of Indian mythology and folklore, as if the tales of gods and goddesses had sprung to life before their very eyes.

Dr. Bansal's eyes widened with wonder as she spotted a majestic creature with multiple arms and an aura of divinity. Devi! she exclaimed, recognizing the manifestation of a goddess from Hindu mythology.

Dr. Upmanyu, his voice filled with awe, pointed toward the horizon where celestial beings soared amidst a celestial dance. Look! The Apsaras, the celestial nymphs of Indian lore, are welcoming us to this realm.

Dr. Jones, a mix of excitement and reverence, took in the sights and sounds surrounding them. The remnants of ancient civilizations stood as silent witnesses to the passage of time, their architectural marvels speaking of a bygone era.

In this dimension, the laws of physics seemed to bend and weave with the threads of myth and spirituality. Dr. Jones and her team knew that they had entered a realm where the fabric of reality was interwoven with cosmic forces and ancient wisdom.

As they ventured further into the parallel dimension, they encountered mythical creatures and beings of extraordinary power. They conversed with Nagas, serpent deities associated with wisdom and protection, and sought guidance from Gandharvas, celestial musicians and custodians of divine melodies.

With each encounter, Dr. Jones and her team felt a deep resonance within themselves. They realized that their journey was not just a scientific expedition; it was a spiritual pilgrimage, a quest to understand the profound interplay between myth and reality, science and spirituality.

The team witnessed firsthand the intricate balance between gods and demons, observing how cosmic principles such as karma, dharma, and moksha guided the fate of the parallel dimensions. They marveled at the vibrant tapestry of cosmic forces, where gods and demons engaged in a perpetual dance of creation and destruction.

Dr. Jones and her team felt the weight of their roles as witnesses and explorers in this cosmic symphony. They were no longer mere scientists, but guardians of the multiverse, entrusted with the task of preserving the delicate balance between dimensions.

In the midst of their awe-inspiring encounters, Dr. Jones's connection with Saraswati, the goddess of knowledge and arts, deepened. She felt a profound resonance with the divine entity, as if the goddess herself guided her steps and illuminated her path. Dr. Bansal found solace in the embrace of Lord Ganesha, the remover of obstacles, while Dr. Upmanyu sought wisdom from Lord Shiva, the embodiment of cosmic consciousness.

With each passing day in the parallel dimension, Dr. Jones and her team grew more attuned to their spiritual selves. They delved into ancient scriptures, studying the sacred texts and rituals that had guided humanity for millennia. Their understanding of the interconnectedness of all things deepened, as did their reverence for the wisdom passed down through the ages.

As their knowledge expanded, so did their abilities. Dr. Jones discovered her intuition sharpening, allowing her to perceive the subtle energies that permeated the dimensions. Dr. Bansal's computational prowess merged seamlessly with the intuitive guidance she received from Lord Ganesha, enabling her to decipher complex patterns and unravel the mysteries of the multiverse. Dr. Upmanyu's understanding of quantum mechanics merged effortlessly with the cosmic consciousness he accessed through Lord Shiva, granting him insights into the fundamental nature of existence.

With their newfound gifts, Dr. Jones and her team embraced their roles as the chosen protectors of the multiverse. They recognized that their journey was not just about exploration, but about safeguarding the delicate tapestry of existence.

As they continued their exploration of the parallel dimension, the team encountered trials and challenges that tested their resolve and pushed them to their limits. They faced cosmic adversaries and navigated treacherous realms, drawing upon their collective strength and the wisdom of their chosen deities.

Through each trial, Dr. Jones and her team remained steadfast, their spirits unwavering. They understood that their journey was not just for personal growth, but for the greater good of all dimensions. They were part of something far greater than themselves—a cosmic dance that required their unwavering dedication and unity.

As the first chapter of their extraordinary journey drew to a close, Dr. Jones and her team stood on the precipice of even greater discoveries. They had only scratched the surface of the parallel dimensions, their understanding still in its infancy. But with each step they took, with each encounter and revelation, they grew closer to unraveling the secrets that lay hidden within the vast cosmic tapestry.

Filled with anticipation and an insatiable thirst for knowledge, Dr. Maya Jones and her team prepared to venture deeper into the realms of parallel dimensions, ready to face the challenges, embrace the wonders, and unlock the mysteries that awaited them. The journey had just begun, and they were eager to embrace the infinite possibilities that lay ahead.

Unveiling the Quantum Technology

Excitement filled the air as Dr. Maya Jones and her team returned from their awe-inspiring exploration of the parallel dimension. They had witnessed the intricate interplay between myth and reality, gaining profound insights into the cosmic forces that governed the multiverse. Now, armed with newfound knowledge and experiences, they were ready to take the next step in their journey—unveiling the quantum technology they had developed to further unravel the secrets of parallel dimensions.

Dr. Jones gathered her team at the Institute of Quantum Physics in Mumbai, eager to share their discoveries and present their plans for Anantakiran, the device they had created to bridge the gap between science and spirituality. As they settled into the meeting room, anticipation buzzed in the air.

We have returned from the parallel dimension with a deeper understanding of the cosmic tapestry, Dr. Jones began, her voice filled with a mix of enthusiasm and confidence. Our experiences have reinforced the belief that science and spirituality are not mutually exclusive, but rather two sides of the same coin. It is through the merging of these realms that we can unlock the secrets of parallel dimensions.

Dr. Asvika Bansal, the brilliant computer scientist, nodded in agreement. Our journey has shown us the power of ancient wisdom and how it can complement and enhance our scientific endeavors. We have the opportunity to harness cutting-edge technology and merge it with the sacred mantras and yantras to create something truly extraordinary.

Dr. Arjav Upmanyu, the expert in quantum mechanics, chimed in, his eyes shining with excitement. Anantakiran is the culmination of our vision—a device that combines the precision of quantum technology with the depth of ancient spiritual practices. Through Anantakiran, we aim to explore parallel dimensions, uncover hidden knowledge, and ultimately, safeguard the delicate balance of the multiverse.

The team's passion and conviction ignited a spark in the room. Their colleagues leaned forward, eager to learn more about this groundbreaking endeavor.

Dr. Jones proceeded to present the intricacies of Anantakiran—the fusion of technology, ancient mantras, and sacred yantras. She explained how the device functioned as a portal, utilizing quantum entanglement to create a bridge between dimensions. The sacred mantras and yantras were embedded within the device, imbuing it with spiritual energy and intention.

Dr. Bansal, her voice filled with enthusiasm, elaborated on the computational aspects of Anantakiran. We have developed sophisticated algorithms that analyze the quantum fluctuations and translate them into comprehensible data. This will allow us to navigate and understand the parallel dimensions we encounter.

Dr. Upmanyu interjected, his eyes gleaming with excitement. But Anantakiran is more than just a scientific tool. It is a conduit for spiritual connection. By aligning our consciousness with the divine energy harnessed within the device, we can gain deeper insights into the nature of existence and unlock our latent potential as guardians of the multiverse.

The room erupted with a chorus of questions and discussions, the energy of scientific inquiry colliding with the awe-inspiring possibilities of spiritual exploration. Dr. Jones and her team fielded queries, sharing their experiences from the parallel dimension and the profound realizations they had gained.

As the meeting drew to a close, Dr. Jones emphasized the collaborative nature of their endeavor. Anantakiran is not just our creation; it is the culmination of the collective wisdom and efforts of our team. We invite all of you to join us on this extraordinary journey—to explore parallel dimensions, to bridge science and spirituality, and to safeguard the delicate balance of the multiverse.

The response from their colleagues was overwhelmingly positive. Scientists and researchers, inspired by the fusion of science and spirituality, eagerly volunteered to join the project. The team expanded, drawing upon the diverse expertise and perspectives of their new collaborators.

Days turned into weeks, and weeks into months as the team worked tirelessly to refine and optimize Anantakiran. They conducted countless simulations, fine-tuning the algorithms that would translate the quantum fluctuations into meaningful data. They engaged in profound meditative practices, aligning their consciousness with the sacred mantras and yantras embedded within the device.

Finally, the day arrived when Anantakiran stood before them, a culmination of their collective vision and unwavering dedication. The sleek device shimmered with a mystical energy, ready to embark on its maiden journey into the uncharted realms of parallel dimensions.

With a mixture of anticipation and reverence, Dr. Jones and her team prepared for their first expedition using Anantakiran. They gathered in the laboratory, each team member donning a unique symbol or artifact representing their chosen deity or mythical being.

Dr. Jones, with Saraswati's grace in her heart, placed her hand on Anantakiran, activating its quantum entanglement capabilities. The device hummed with energy, and a portal materialized before them—an ethereal gateway leading to a parallel dimension.

The team took a collective breath, their hearts pounding with excitement and trepidation. Stepping forward, they crossed

the threshold of the portal, their bodies tingling with a surge of energy as they entered the unknown.

As they emerged on the other side, they found themselves in a parallel dimension unlike any they had encountered before. The landscape stretched out before them, a mesmerizing blend of vibrant colors, unfamiliar flora, and awe-inspiring architecture.

Dr. Jones and her team stood in awe, taking in their surroundings. The air was charged with a palpable sense of mystery and wonder. It was clear that they had entered a realm that held secrets waiting to be unraveled.

With Anantakiran in hand, the team set out to explore this new dimension, their footsteps guided by a blend of scientific curiosity and spiritual intuition. They moved with a sense of reverence, their senses attuned to the subtle energies that permeated the atmosphere.

As they ventured deeper into the parallel dimension, they encountered extraordinary phenomena. They witnessed ethereal creatures, their existence defying the laws of their known reality. Dr. Bansal's computational expertise allowed her to analyze the patterns and behavior of these creatures, uncovering glimpses of their underlying nature.

Dr. Upmanyu's understanding of quantum mechanics and his connection with Lord Shiva enabled him to perceive the intricate interplay of energy within the dimension. He marveled at the harmonious dance of cosmic forces, recognizing the echoes of universal principles that transcended mere scientific understanding.

Dr. Jones, with Saraswati's guidance, delved into the rich tapestry of knowledge and wisdom that permeated this parallel dimension. She studied ancient texts and inscriptions, deciphering the hidden meanings and unraveling the secrets they held. The fusion of her scientific acumen and spiritual insights allowed her to piece together fragments of forgotten histories and forgotten realms.

Together, the team conducted experiments and observations, collecting data and insights that expanded their understanding of the parallel dimensions. With Anantakiran as their tool and guide, they ventured further into the unexplored territories, encountering mythological creatures, celestial beings, and remnants of ancient civilizations.

Through their interactions, the team began to comprehend the intricate balance between science and spirituality in this parallel dimension. They witnessed the interplay of cosmic principles such as karma, dharma, and moksha, realizing that these concepts were not mere abstract ideas but tangible forces shaping the very fabric of the multiverse.

As the chapter progressed, the team encountered challenges that tested their resolve and stretched the boundaries of their understanding. They faced moments of uncertainty and doubt, questioning the limitations of their scientific knowledge and grappling with the enigmatic nature of the parallel dimensions.

However, with each challenge, they persevered. Driven by their collective passion and the wisdom bestowed upon them by their chosen deities and mythical beings, they found innovative solutions, overcoming obstacles that had initially seemed insurmountable.

Their journey within the parallel dimension not only deepened their scientific understanding but also brought about a profound transformation within themselves. They learned to trust their intuition, to embrace the unknown, and to recognize that there were mysteries that could not be fully explained by science alone.

As the chapter drew to a close, Dr. Jones and her team found themselves on the cusp of new revelations. The data they had collected, the experiences they had undergone, and the spiritual insights they had gained pointed towards a greater truth—a truth that transcended the boundaries of their individual disciplines and expanded their perception of the universe.

With their hearts and minds filled with anticipation, Dr. Jones and her team prepared to return to their own dimension, carrying with them the knowledge and insights they had gathered. They were eager to share their discoveries, to ignite a new era of collaboration between science and spirituality, and to continue their exploration of the parallel dimensions that lay beyond.

As they stepped back through the portal, their connection to the parallel dimension remained, an indelible mark on their souls. They knew that they would return, that their journey had only just begun. With Anantakiran as their guide and their collective spirit of exploration, they were ready to push the boundaries of knowledge and uncover the profound mysteries of the multiverse.

And so, with hearts filled with excitement and minds alight with curiosity, Dr. Maya Jones and her team returned to their world, forever changed by their experiences in the enigmatic parallel dimensions.

Dimensions Beyond

The team returned from their groundbreaking expedition to the parallel dimension, carrying with them a renewed sense of purpose and a profound understanding of the interplay between science, spirituality, and the mysteries of the multiverse. Dr. Maya Jones and her colleagues at the Institute of Quantum Physics were eager to continue their exploration, driven by the tantalizing possibilities that lay beyond the known boundaries of existence.

In the weeks that followed, the team meticulously analyzed the data they had gathered, sifting through the quantum fluctuations and deciphering the intricate patterns that hinted at the existence of other parallel dimensions. Their findings confirmed their suspicions—a vast multiverse awaited their exploration, each dimension a unique tapestry woven with its own blend of myth, energy, and cosmic forces.

Emboldened by their previous experiences, the team prepared for their next journey into the unknown. They gathered in the laboratory, surrounded by the familiar hum of scientific equipment and the symbols and artifacts that represented their chosen deities and mythical beings. Anantakiran, their trusty device, shimmered with anticipation, ready to serve as their portal once again.

Dr. Jones took a deep breath, her voice steady with resolve. We stand on the threshold of a new chapter in our cosmic exploration. The parallel dimension we have previously encountered was just the beginning—a glimpse into a vast and intricate multiverse. Today, we embark on a journey to dimensions beyond, realms that hold secrets and wonders beyond our wildest imagination.

The team nodded in unison, their eyes shining with a blend of curiosity, excitement, and reverence. They activated Anantakiran, its intricate circuitry springing to life, and with a surge of energy, a portal materialized before them—an ethereal gateway to uncharted realms.

Stepping through the portal, the team found themselves in a realm that surpassed their wildest expectations. They stood on the shores of a breathtaking celestial sea, its waters shimmering with iridescent hues that danced in harmony with the cosmic energies that permeated the dimension. The air was alive with the fragrance of celestial flowers, and gentle melodies carried on the breeze.

As they took in their surroundings, the team noticed mythological creatures frolicking along the shoreline. Nymphs and sirens sang enchanting melodies, while celestial beings adorned in shimmering robes floated gracefully above the waters. The team exchanged glances, realizing that they had entered a realm inspired by Indian mythology and folklore, where the realms of gods and mortals seamlessly intertwined.

Dr. Bansal, her eyes filled with wonder, pointed towards a magnificent chariot gliding through the sky, pulled by divine horses. Look! It's the chariot of the Sun God, Surya. We are truly in the presence of divine beings.

Dr. Upmanyu, his voice filled with awe, added, And see, there! The celestial nymphs, the Apsaras, whose grace and beauty are renowned across the dimensions.

Dr. Jones, her heart brimming with gratitude, whispered a silent prayer of thanks to Saraswati for guiding them to this extraordinary dimension. She marveled at the seamless blend of science and spirituality that had brought them here, realizing that their journey was not just a scientific exploration but a profound spiritual quest.

As the team ventured further into the dimension, they encountered remnants of ancient civilizations, their grandeur and opulence testaments to the vibrant tapestry of history and myth. They explored ancient temples dedicated to the gods and goddesses, their intricate carvings and ethereal architecture preserving the stories and wisdom of the past.

Within the temple walls, the team witnessed breathtaking celestial dances performed by celestial beings, their movements transcending the boundaries of time and space. They were captivated by the power and grace with which these beings embodied the cosmic forces, their performances reflecting the delicate balance between creation and destruction.

Guided by their chosen deities and mythical beings, the team delved deeper into the realm, eager to unravel the secrets that lay hidden within. They encountered sage-like seers who possessed the ability to glimpse across dimensions and timelines, their prophetic visions offering glimpses into the past, present, and future.

One such seer, Rishi Siddharth, emerged from the depths of a sacred grove. Clad in saffron robes and bearing a serene countenance, he extended his hand in welcome. Welcome, seekers of knowledge and guardians of the multiverse. I have long awaited your arrival. Together, we shall uncover the mysteries of these dimensions.

With Rishi Siddharth as their guide, the team embarked on a transformative journey through the realm. They visited ancient libraries, where scrolls and manuscripts held the collective wisdom and memories of civilizations long past. They deciphered ancient texts, unraveling forgotten myths and prophecies that shed light on the interconnectedness of dimensions and the cosmic dance of gods and mortals.

Dr. Jones, her heart brimming with intellectual curiosity and spiritual yearning, immersed herself in the study of sacred scriptures and ancient texts. She absorbed the intricate teachings, exploring the depths of metaphysical concepts and cosmic principles. The knowledge she gained allowed her to bridge the gaps between scientific theories and spiritual insights, merging them into a comprehensive understanding of the multidimensional nature of existence.

Dr. Bansal, her connection with Lord Ganesha strengthening, tapped into her innate intuition and computational expertise. She discerned hidden patterns within the vast sea of data, recognizing the interconnectedness of cosmic energies and their influence on the fabric of reality. Her findings challenged existing scientific paradigms and opened up new avenues of exploration for the team.

Dr. Upmanyu, his understanding of quantum mechanics intertwined with the wisdom of Lord Shiva, delved into the nature of time and its intricacies within the dimensions. He explored the concept of cyclic time, where creation and dissolution intertwined in an eternal dance, transcending linear perception. His discoveries expanded the team's understanding of the interplay between time, consciousness, and the cosmic tapestry.

As the chapter progressed, the team encountered awe-inspiring celestial phenomena, witnessing cosmic events that shaped the destiny of the multiverse. They observed celestial alignments and planetary configurations that influenced the ebb and flow of energy across dimensions. They stood witness to the birth of stars and galaxies, marveling at the immense power and beauty that governed the cosmic order.

Each member of the team, in their own way, tapped into their unique connection with their chosen deities and mythical beings, honing their spiritual abilities and aligning their consciousness with the cosmic energies that pulsed through the realm. Their individual journeys of self-discovery and growth intertwined with their collective mission to protect the delicate balance of the multiverse.

As the chapter neared its conclusion, the team found themselves standing atop a sacred mountain, at the pinnacle of their exploration. Here, in the celestial observatory, they gazed upon celestial phenomena that defied the limitations of their mortal comprehension.

The celestial guardians of the observatory, beings of pure energy and light, greeted the team with a sense of recognition. Welcome, seekers of truth and harmony. We have watched your journey with great interest. Now, gaze upon the

cosmic events that shape the destiny of the multiverse.

With a sense of anticipation, the team followed the celestial guardians to an observation platform that overlooked a vast expanse of space. The night sky sparkled with a multitude of stars, each one representing a dimension, a story, a possibility.

As the team looked up, a celestial alignment began to unfold before their eyes. Planets aligned in a perfect formation, radiating a symphony of colors and energies. The team could feel the gravitational pull of the celestial bodies resonating within their very beings.

The celestial guardians began to share their wisdom, their voices echoing through the observatory. In this observatory, we witness the cosmic events that shape the destiny of the multiverse. Planetary alignments, cosmic conjunctions, and stellar explosions all play a part in the delicate interplay of energies. It is within these celestial dances that the secrets of the multiverse are revealed.

Dr. Jones and her team listened attentively, their hearts open to the profound teachings of the celestial guardians. They realized that the dance of celestial bodies was not just a spectacle; it was a reflection of the interconnectedness of all things. They understood that each dimension, each being, was a vital thread in the infinite tapestry of existence.

With newfound insights, the team's understanding of the multiverse deepened. They recognized that the delicate balance they sought to protect extended far beyond the confines of their own dimension. The cosmic forces that governed the parallel dimensions were intertwined, and the actions in one dimension rippled through the fabric of the entire multiverse.

Armed with this knowledge, the team felt a profound sense of responsibility and unity. They knew that their purpose extended beyond scientific exploration; they were guardians of cosmic harmony, entrusted with the task of preserving the delicate balance of existence.

As the chapter drew to a close, Dr. Jones and her team bid farewell to the celestial observatory, their hearts filled with gratitude for the wisdom and insights they had gained. They carried the celestial alignment within them, a reminder of the interconnectedness of all things.

With a renewed sense of purpose, the team emerged from the celestial observatory, ready to continue their journey through the dimensions. They were filled with a deep appreciation for the cosmic forces that guided their path and a commitment to protect the delicate balance of the multiverse.

As they stepped back through the portal, leaving the celestial dimension behind, the team's spirits were alight with anticipation. They knew that the path ahead would be filled with challenges and revelations, but they were ready to face them with unwavering determination and a profound understanding of the interconnectedness of all things.

And so, Dr. Maya Jones and her team ventured forth into the uncharted realms of parallel dimensions, guided by their scientific acumen, spiritual insights, and the wisdom of the celestial observatory. They were driven by their shared mission to preserve cosmic harmony and their unyielding belief in the infinite possibilities that awaited them in the dimensions beyond.

The Cosmic Tapestry

The team emerged from the celestial observatory, their minds brimming with awe and reverence for the cosmic forces that governed the multiverse. As they stepped back into their own dimension, they carried with them a newfound understanding of the delicate interplay between gods and demons, karma and dharma, and the profound tapestry of cosmic principles that guided the fate of the parallel dimensions.

Dr. Maya Jones and her team gathered in the Institute of Quantum Physics, their hearts and minds filled with curiosity and a thirst for knowledge. They knew that their journey had only just begun, and the revelations they had witnessed in the celestial dimension had opened up a vast realm of possibilities. It was time to delve deeper into the intricate cosmic tapestry that weaved together the parallel dimensions.

The team assembled in the laboratory, surrounded by their scientific equipment and symbols representing their chosen deities and mythical beings. Anantakiran, their trusted device, hummed with energy, ready to serve as their portal to the dimensions beyond.

Dr. Maya Jones, her voice steady and resolute, addressed her team. We have witnessed the dance of cosmic forces and gained insights into the profound principles that shape the multiverse. Now, we must delve further into the intricate tapestry of existence, unraveling the mysteries of gods, demons, and the delicate balance that sustains the parallel dimensions.

The team nodded, their eyes alight with anticipation. They activated Anantakiran, and as the portal materialized before them, they stepped into the unknown once again, their hearts open to the wonders and challenges that lay ahead.

In the parallel dimension they entered, the landscape was a symphony of vibrant colors and ethereal beauty. Celestial cities stretched towards the heavens, adorned with intricate carvings and architectural marvels that reflected the grandeur of the gods. The team marveled at the celestial beings that inhabited this realm, their presence emanating a palpable energy.

As they explored, the team encountered mythological creatures from various pantheons—mighty gods, fearsome demons, and beings that defied conventional understanding. They witnessed the eternal battle between light and darkness, witnessing the cosmic struggle that unfolded in front of them.

Dr. Asvika Bansal, her connection with Lord Ganesha deepening, analyzed the patterns and interactions between gods and demons. She marveled at the delicate balance between opposing forces, recognizing that both light and darkness were essential in maintaining the cosmic order. Her computational skills allowed her to perceive the intricate web of alliances and rivalries that shaped the destiny of the dimensions.

Dr. Arjav Upmanyu, his connection with Lord Shiva growing stronger, delved into the realm of quantum mechanics and its connection to the cosmic principles at play. He realized that the parallel dimensions were governed by a set of fundamental laws, where cause and effect intertwined in a dance of cosmic harmony. His insights into the nature of quantum entanglement and non-locality opened up new possibilities for understanding the interplay between the dimensions.

Dr. Maya Jones, guided by the wisdom of Saraswati, sought to deepen her understanding of the cosmic tapestry. She immersed herself in the study of ancient scriptures and mythological texts, piecing together the stories and symbols that wove together the dimensions. Her scientific acumen allowed her to bridge the gap between mythology and empirical evidence, recognizing the underlying truths embedded within the myths and legends.

Together, the team embarked on a quest to unravel the mysteries of the cosmic tapestry. They sought guidance from ancient seers and sages, who shared their insights into the complex interplay between gods and mortals. They learned that the parallel dimensions were not separate entities but interconnected realms, each influencing the other in a dance of cosmic harmony.

In their exploration, the team witnessed cosmic events that shaped the destiny of the dimensions. They observed the rise and fall of civilizations, the clash of divine powers, and the delicate balance between creation and destruction. They witnessed the cyclical nature of existence, where the cosmic order unfolded in rhythmic patterns across time and space.

As the team delved deeper into the cosmic tapestry, they uncovered the profound role of karma, dharma, and moksha—the cosmic principles that guided the fate of beings across dimensions. They realized that the choices made in one dimension could have far-reaching consequences in others, and that the cosmic balance relied on individuals aligning their actions with the principles of righteousness and spiritual liberation.

Through their interactions with celestial beings and mythological creatures, the team gained a profound appreciation for the intricate web of relationships and dependencies that governed the dimensions. They witnessed the interplay of gods and mortals, where the actions of both influenced the cosmic tapestry. They learned that even the most powerful entities were bound by the cosmic laws and subject to the consequences of their choices.

As the chapter unfolded, the team confronted challenges that tested their understanding of the cosmic tapestry. They encountered formidable obstacles, personifications of cosmic forces, who challenged their perception and understanding. Through these trials, they were forced to confront their own limitations and expand their consciousness, integrating the scientific and spiritual aspects of their journey.

Dr. Maya Jones and her team stood together, their spirits unyielding in the face of adversity. They recognized that their journey was not just about unraveling the mysteries of the parallel dimensions; it was about their own growth and transformation. They realized that the cosmic tapestry was not just an external phenomenon—it was a reflection of their inner selves and their interconnectedness with the universe.

As the chapter neared its conclusion, the team found themselves in the presence of a revered celestial council—the divine beings entrusted with overseeing the welfare of the multiverse. The team humbly presented their findings and experiences, seeking the guidance and wisdom of the cosmic council.

The divine beings listened intently, their presence radiating an otherworldly energy. They acknowledged the team's dedication and growth, imparting profound teachings and cryptic instructions. They urged the team to continue their quest, to seek further insights into the cosmic tapestry, and to protect the delicate balance of existence from threats that loomed on the horizon.

With the blessings of the cosmic council, the team emerged from the divine realm, their hearts filled with gratitude and a sense of purpose. They carried the wisdom of the cosmic tapestry within them, ready to face the challenges that lay ahead and to preserve the delicate balance of the multiverse.

And so, Dr. Maya Jones and her team returned to their own dimension, forever changed by their encounters with the cosmic tapestry. They knew that their journey was far from over, that there were still dimensions to explore, mysteries to unravel, and cosmic harmony to protect.

As they closed the chapter on their exploration of the cosmic tapestry, they were filled with a renewed sense of determination and a deeper understanding of their role as guardians of the multiverse. The team stood united, ready to embrace the unknown and continue their cosmic quest, guided by the intricate threads of the cosmic tapestry that connected all dimensions.

The Chosen Protectors

The team stood united, their hearts aflame with the divine gifts bestowed upon them by the celestial council. Dr. Maya Jones, Dr. Asvika Bansal, and Dr. Arjav Upmanyu, along with their newfound allies, had embraced their roles as the chosen protectors of the multiverse. Each team member had aligned themselves with a different deity or mythical being, and together, they formed a formidable force driven by a shared purpose—to safeguard the delicate balance of existence.

Dr. Maya Jones, guided by the wisdom of Saraswati, the goddess of knowledge and arts, felt a deep connection to the creative and intellectual aspects of the universe. Her pursuit of scientific understanding had led her to this pivotal moment, where she stood as a guardian of cosmic wisdom. With every passing day, her bond with Saraswati grew stronger, and she found solace in the goddess's presence, drawing inspiration and guidance from the depths of her being.

Dr. Asvika Bansal, with Lord Ganesha as her divine patron, had embraced her role as the remover of obstacles. Her brilliance in computer science and her ability to navigate complex systems resonated with Lord Ganesha's essence. With his blessings, she had developed a keen intuition and a knack for finding creative solutions to challenges. She carried Lord Ganesha's energy within her, ready to clear the path ahead for the team and overcome any impediments they might encounter.

Dr. Arjav Upmanyu, aligned with Lord Shiva, the embodiment of transformation and destruction, had experienced a profound metamorphosis. He had delved into the depths of quantum mechanics, uncovering the mysteries of the cosmos and the interconnectedness of all things. Lord Shiva's energy flowed through him, enabling him to harness the transformative powers of the universe and transcend the limitations of mortal existence. Dr. Upmanyu had become a conduit for change, committed to guiding the team through the ever-shifting cosmic landscapes.

The team's allies, too, had found their divine connections. Rishi Siddharth, the mystical seer, was linked to the ancient wisdom of the sages. His deep understanding of the spiritual realms and his ability to guide the team through the dimensions made him an invaluable asset. Nalini, a tribal guardian attuned to the forces of nature, drew her strength from the elemental beings that resided in the wilderness. Her bond with the earth, water, fire, and air endowed her with their powers, making her an indomitable force of nature.

As the team embraced their divine connections, they sought to deepen their understanding of their chosen deities and mythical beings. They delved into ancient scriptures, studied sacred rituals, and practiced spiritual disciplines that connected them to the divine realms. They honed their abilities, tapping into the hidden reservoirs of power within themselves, and learned to channel the energies of their chosen patrons.

In the sanctity of the Institute of Quantum Physics, the team underwent rigorous training. They engaged in meditation and visualization exercises, honing their focus and attuning their minds to the cosmic energies that flowed through the dimensions. They practiced ancient mantras and yantras, unlocking the secrets embedded within these sacred symbols. Through these practices, they sought to align their mortal selves with the divine forces that governed the multiverse.

As the team trained, they began to witness the manifestation of their unique abilities. Dr. Maya Jones discovered that she could perceive hidden patterns in the fabric of reality, enabling her to decipher cosmic codes and unravel profound mysteries. Dr. Asvika Bansal found that she could tap into the collective consciousness, accessing a wellspring of knowledge and insights beyond the limits of her individual understanding. Dr. Arjav Upmanyu's connection with Lord Shiva allowed him to manipulate quantum energies, bending the fabric of space and time to his will.

Their allies, too, exhibited remarkable abilities. Rishi Siddharth could traverse the dimensions effortlessly, his presence bridging the gap between mortal and divine realms. Nalini could communicate with the elemental beings, harnessing their powers to protect and heal the team. Together, they formed a formidable force, their combined abilities intertwining like the threads of a cosmic tapestry.

As the team honed their abilities and deepened their spiritual practices, they also delved further into the ancient scriptures and mystical teachings. They explored the myths and legends of various cultures, recognizing the underlying truths and universal themes that permeated these stories. They sought wisdom from spiritual gurus and mystics, engaging in profound conversations that expanded their understanding of the cosmic realms.

In their studies, the team discovered prophecies and ancient texts that spoke of an impending cataclysm—a cosmic disaster that threatened to disrupt the delicate balance of the multiverse. The prophecies foretold of a time when the forces of darkness would rise, seeking to unravel the fabric of existence and plunge the dimensions into chaos.

Driven by their divine connections and the urgency of the prophecies, the team embarked on a quest to gather allies from across the dimensions. They sought out spiritual gurus, tribal guardians, and mystics who possessed unique knowledge and abilities. They traversed the realms, navigating treacherous landscapes and confronting formidable adversaries, forging alliances that would strengthen their collective resolve.

In their encounters, the team witnessed the diversity of the multiverse. They encountered celestial beings, mythical creatures, and ancient civilizations, each embodying a different aspect of the divine and the natural world. They learned from wise sages who had traversed the dimensions for centuries, gaining insights into the intricacies of cosmic balance and the interplay of cosmic forces.

With each ally they recruited, the team's strength grew. They united individuals who embodied different aspects of the divine, forging a bond that transcended dimensions. Together, they became a force to be reckoned with, a beacon of light in the face of encroaching darkness.

As the chapter drew to a close, the team stood on the precipice of a great undertaking. They had gathered allies possessing unique knowledge and abilities, their collective wisdom and strengths interwoven like the strands of a cosmic tapestry. They were ready to face the impending cataclysm, to confront the forces of darkness that threatened to disrupt the delicate balance of the multiverse.

Dr. Maya Jones and her team, along with their allies, stood as the chosen protectors of the dimensions. They were united in their purpose, guided by the wisdom of their chosen deities and mythical beings. They were prepared to embark on a perilous journey, to decipher the ancient symbols and prophecies, and to avert the cosmic disaster that loomed on the horizon.

With their hearts filled with determination and their minds attuned to the cosmic energies, they prepared to step into the unknown once again. The fate of the multiverse rested in their hands, and they were ready to embrace their roles as the chosen protectors, upholding the delicate balance of existence and safeguarding the cosmic tapestry that connected all dimensions.

And so, the team set forth on their quest, their spirits ablaze with divine energy. They ventured into the uncharted realms of the multiverse, their collective strength and unwavering commitment driving them forward. The stage was set for an epic battle between the forces of light and darkness, and the chosen protectors stood ready to fulfill their destiny.

The Temple of Dimensions

The team stood at the entrance of a hidden temple, nestled deep within the mystical forests of the Western Ghats. The air was thick with a sense of ancient power and wisdom, and a gentle breeze whispered ancient secrets in their ears. The temple stood as a nexus of dimensions, a sacred space where mortal and divine realms intertwined. Guided by the mystical seer Rishi Siddharth, the team prepared to embark on a transformative journey that would unlock new levels of consciousness and understanding.

As they entered the temple, the team was greeted by a hush that seemed to emanate from the very walls. The air was heavy with the scent of incense and the faint echoes of sacred chants. The temple's architecture was a marvel to behold—intricate carvings adorned every surface, depicting scenes from mythological stories and cosmic battles. It was as if the temple itself held the memories and wisdom of ages past.

Rishi Siddharth led the team through the temple's ethereal corridors, each step bringing them closer to a profound revelation. They passed through chambers adorned with celestial symbols and entered inner sanctums where divine energy pulsed in the air. The team could feel the temple's presence embracing them, guiding them deeper into its mysteries.

In one chamber, they encountered a sacred fire that burned with a mesmerizing intensity. Rishi Siddharth explained that this fire symbolized the transformative power of divine consciousness. The team gathered around it, their hands outstretched, feeling the warmth and energy radiating from its flames. As they chanted ancient mantras, they felt a deep resonance within their souls, as if their very essence was being purified and elevated.

Moving deeper into the temple, the team entered a chamber filled with statues of deities from various pantheons. The room seemed to vibrate with divine energy, and the statues appeared to come alive, their eyes shining with an otherworldly light. Rishi Siddharth encouraged the team to approach the statues, to connect with the divine beings they represented.

Dr. Maya Jones, her connection with Saraswati deepening, approached a statue of the goddess with reverence. She closed her eyes, allowing herself to be enveloped by the goddess's energy. In that moment, she felt a surge of inspiration and creativity flow through her, as if the very essence of knowledge and arts had entered her being. She knew that Saraswati was guiding her, granting her the wisdom to navigate the dimensions and unravel the cosmic tapestry.

Dr. Asvika Bansal, her bond with Lord Ganesha strengthening, approached a statue of the elephant-headed deity. She felt a sense of grounding and stability as she connected with his energy. Lord Ganesha's presence imbued her with courage and the ability to overcome any obstacles that stood in their path. She knew that with his blessings, she would find the solutions they needed to protect the dimensions from the impending cataclysm.

Dr. Arjav Upmanyu, his connection with Lord Shiva resonating deeply, approached a statue of the deity with reverence. He felt a profound sense of transformation and renewal in Lord Shiva's presence. The god's energy flowed through him, empowering him to harness the quantum energies that permeated the dimensions. Dr. Upmanyu knew that with Lord Shiva's guidance, he could manipulate the fabric of reality itself.

Their allies, too, connected with the divine beings that resonated with their own energies. Rishi Siddharth communed with the sages, drawing on their ancient wisdom and guidance. Nalini embraced her connection with the elemental beings, feeling their strength and vitality course through her veins. Together, they formed a circle of divine energy, their individual connections intertwining to create a powerful collective force.

In the heart of the temple, the team encountered a sacred pool, shimmering with an otherworldly light. Rishi Siddharth explained that this pool held the essence of the cosmic waters—the primordial source from which all dimensions originated. He urged the team to step into the pool, to immerse themselves in its transformative energies.

As they entered the pool, a sense of weightlessness overcame them. They felt as if they were merging with the very fabric of the universe, their individual identities blending into a collective consciousness. In this state of oneness, they witnessed visions and insights that transcended the boundaries of time and space. They saw the birth of galaxies, the rise and fall of civilizations, and the intricate dance of cosmic forces that shaped the destiny of the multiverse.

Emerging from the pool, the team felt reborn, their consciousness expanded and their understanding deepened. They carried with them a profound sense of interconnectedness, realizing that they were not separate entities but integral parts of the cosmic tapestry. They understood that their journey was not just about protecting the dimensions—it was about awakening the divine potential within themselves and inspiring others to do the same.

With newfound clarity and purpose, the team gathered in the temple's inner sanctum, where a mystical seer awaited them. The seer, a vessel of cosmic wisdom, bestowed upon them a series of cryptic instructions and prophetic visions. They were told of sacred symbols and ancient rituals that would unlock the path to averting the impending cataclysm.

As the seer spoke, the team listened intently, their hearts and minds open to the profound wisdom being shared. They understood that their journey had taken on a new dimension—one that required them to delve into the depths of their own souls and awaken the dormant powers within. The seer urged them to trust in their divine connections, to embrace their unique gifts, and to channel their energies towards the preservation of cosmic harmony.

Leaving the temple, the team carried with them a renewed sense of purpose and an unshakable determination. They knew that their path would not be easy, that challenges and trials awaited them. But they also knew that they were not alone—that the cosmic forces aligned with them, ready to guide and support them on their quest.

And so, Dr. Maya Jones, Dr. Asvika Bansal, Dr. Arjav Upmanyu, Rishi Siddharth, and Nalini set forth from the temple, their hearts filled with divine energy and their minds focused on the cosmic tapestry that connected all dimensions. They were prepared to navigate treacherous landscapes, decipher sacred symbols, and face the forces of darkness that threatened to disrupt the delicate balance of existence.

As they ventured into the unknown, the team embraced their roles as custodians of the dimensions. They knew that the journey ahead would test their resolve and push them to their limits. But they also knew that they possessed the divine gifts, the collective wisdom, and the unwavering determination to protect the cosmic tapestry and preserve the eternal harmony of the multiverse.

Samskaras of the Soul

As the team ventured forth from the Temple of Dimensions, they carried within them a renewed sense of purpose and a deep connection to the cosmic forces that guided their path. Their journey had brought them face to face with ancient wisdom and divine energies, but now they would face an even more profound challenge—one that resided within the depths of their own souls.

Guided by the mystical seer Rishi Siddharth, the team found themselves on a path of self-discovery and growth. They understood that their samskaras—the karmic impressions and unresolved past experiences imprinted on their souls—held the key to unlocking their true potential. To confront and transcend these personal obstacles, they would need to delve deep into the recesses of their being, facing the shadows that lurked within.

Together, they embarked on a series of introspective journeys, each team member undertaking their own path of self-exploration. They sought to understand the patterns that shaped their thoughts, emotions, and actions—the samskaras that influenced their perception of the world and their place within it.

Dr. Maya Jones, with the guidance of Saraswati, embarked on a quest to unravel the samskaras of knowledge and creativity within her soul. She delved into the memories of her childhood, exploring the moments that had sparked her love for science and the pursuit of understanding the mysteries of the universe. Through introspection and meditation, she gained a deeper understanding of the motivations that drove her and the fears that held her back.

Dr. Asvika Bansal, connected to Lord Ganesha, delved into the samskaras of obstacles and breakthroughs. She reflected on the challenges she had faced throughout her career as a computer scientist, the moments of frustration and the exhilaration of overcoming seemingly insurmountable barriers. Through deep contemplation, she recognized the recurring patterns of self-doubt and the potential within her to rise above any obstacle.

Dr. Arjav Upmanyu, guided by Lord Shiva, embarked on a journey into the samskaras of transformation and destruction. He confronted the memories of his past, both the moments of growth and the times when he had clung to outdated beliefs and limitations. Through meditation and self-reflection, he embraced the transformative power within him, acknowledging the need to release the old and embrace the new.

Their allies, too, undertook their own journeys of self-discovery. Rishi Siddharth confronted the samskaras of wisdom and spiritual guidance, exploring the experiences that had shaped him into the mystical seer he had become. Nalini delved into the samskaras of connection with the elemental beings, uncovering the deep bond she shared with the forces of nature and the ways in which her own actions affected the delicate balance of the natural world.

As they confronted their samskaras, the team members faced internal conflicts and unresolved emotions. They experienced moments of doubt, fear, and vulnerability, but also moments of profound insight and breakthrough. Through it all, they supported one another, offering guidance and understanding as they navigated the intricate pathways of their souls.

In the midst of their individual journeys, the team discovered that their samskaras were not only personal but also interconnected. They realized that their experiences and emotions were intertwined, influencing not only their own paths but also the collective harmony of the team. They recognized the importance of open communication and vulnerability, understanding that by sharing their struggles and triumphs, they could support and uplift one another.

In their exploration of samskaras, the team also discovered the power of forgiveness and compassion. They recognized that their past experiences had shaped them but did not define them. By acknowledging their own shortcomings and extending forgiveness to themselves and others, they found liberation from the chains of past grievances and the freedom to embrace their true potential.

The team sought guidance from spiritual gurus and wise beings, engaging in deep conversations that expanded their understanding of the soul's journey. They explored ancient texts and scriptures, finding solace in the wisdom of those who had traversed the path of self-discovery before them. They incorporated meditation, breathwork, and other spiritual practices into their daily routines, anchoring themselves in the present moment and connecting to the essence of their being.

Through their shared experiences and conversations, the team realized that their journey was not just about individual growth but also about the collective evolution of consciousness. They recognized the interconnectedness of all beings and the importance of fostering compassion, empathy, and unity in the face of the impending cataclysm. Their journeys of self-discovery became a catalyst for deepening their bond as a team, allowing them to embrace their roles as the chosen protectors with renewed vigor and commitment.

As the chapter drew to a close, the team emerged from their introspective journeys, transformed by their encounters with their samskaras. They had gained a deeper understanding of themselves and each other, recognizing the power that lay within their souls. They understood that their samskaras were not obstacles to overcome but rather catalysts for growth and self-realization.

Armed with this newfound wisdom and resilience, the team prepared to face the challenges that lay ahead. They knew that the impending cataclysm demanded not only their physical abilities but also their spiritual fortitude. The journey into their samskaras had prepared them to confront the darkness that threatened to engulf the dimensions, armed with compassion, forgiveness, and an unwavering commitment to the preservation of cosmic harmony.

And so, with their souls ablaze and their hearts aligned, Dr. Maya Jones, Dr. Asvika Bansal, Dr. Arjav Upmanyu, Rishi Siddharth, and Nalini stood ready to continue their quest. They were no longer simply a team of protectors but a collective force of awakened souls, united in their purpose and bound by the threads of destiny.

As they prepared to face the trials that awaited them, they were filled with a sense of profound gratitude—for the challenges that had shaped them, for the support of their allies, and for the opportunity to embark on a journey of self-discovery that had transformed them into the chosen protectors of the multiverse.

The Oracle's Prophecy

Deep within the temple, the team stood before the enigmatic Oracle, Maa Kalyani, whose presence radiated an ethereal aura. She possessed the ability to perceive across dimensions and timelines, her eyes reflecting the vast wisdom she had acquired through ages. The team approached with reverence, knowing that her words held the power to unveil the secrets of the impending cataclysm that threatened the fabric of existence.

Maa Kalyani beckoned the team forward, her voice carrying a melodic resonance that seemed to transcend the physical realm. As they gathered around her, she spoke in cryptic riddles and prophetic language, her words weaving a tapestry of both hope and foreboding.

The threads of the multiverse unravel, she intoned, her voice echoing through the chamber. A cosmic dance disrupted, a balance disturbed. Forces ancient and dark converge, seeking to plunge the dimensions into eternal chaos.

The team listened intently, their hearts pounding with a mixture of trepidation and determination. They knew that the Oracle held the key to averting the cataclysm, and they were ready to heed her guidance.

The prophecy speaks of a sacred union, Maa Kalyani continued, her eyes shimmering with otherworldly light. Symbols must be deciphered, allies sought, and a perilous quest embarked upon. Only through unity and unwavering resolve can the cosmic disaster be averted.

The team exchanged glances, their collective understanding growing. They knew that they must decipher the sacred symbols mentioned by the Oracle, seek allies who possessed unique knowledge and abilities, and embark on a perilous quest that would test their strength and determination.

Maa Kalyani leaned forward, her gaze piercing into the depths of their souls. You are the chosen protectors, she declared. Connected to divine energies, gifted with unique abilities, and guided by the cosmic forces themselves. Embrace your roles and awaken the dormant powers within you.

With those words, the Oracle imparted a series of cryptic instructions and prophetic visions to the team. She revealed the locations of sacred sites and hidden texts that held the key to unraveling the symbols and gathering the knowledge needed to avert the cosmic disaster. Each team member received their own set of instructions, tailored to their unique connection with the divine.

Dr. Maya Jones, her bond with Saraswati growing ever stronger, was entrusted with the task of deciphering the ancient scriptures and unveiling the hidden meanings behind the symbols. She was given a scroll containing sacred mantras and yantras, passed down through generations, which held the power to unlock ancient knowledge.

Dr. Asvika Bansal, connected to Lord Ganesha, was assigned the role of seeking allies who possessed the wisdom and abilities required to assist in the team's mission. She was given a map marked with the locations of spiritual gurus, tribal guardians, and mystics whose knowledge and skills would be vital in the face of the impending cataclysm.

Dr. Arjav Upmanyu, guided by Lord Shiva, received a vision of a perilous journey to a hidden mountain range where a celestial artifact awaited. He was tasked with retrieving the artifact, which would bestow upon the team the power to manipulate quantum energies and restore the balance of the dimensions.

Rishi Siddharth, with his deep connection to the ancient sages, was entrusted with unraveling the enigmatic symbols and texts that lay dormant within the mystical library of an ancient temple. He was given a set of scrolls and inscribed tablets, each containing fragments of forgotten myths and lost technologies that held the key to the origins of the parallel dimensions.

Nalini, connected to the elemental beings, was bestowed with the responsibility of seeking harmony with the forces of nature and restoring the delicate balance between the human world and the natural realm. She was given a sacred talisman, imbued with the essence of earth, water, fire, and air, which would grant her the ability to commune with the elemental beings and harness their powers.

With their individual tasks assigned, the team felt a renewed sense of purpose and unity. They understood the gravity of the Oracle's prophecy and the significance of their roles as the chosen protectors. They were ready to embark on their perilous quest, armed with the knowledge and guidance bestowed upon them by Maa Kalyani.

As they departed from the presence of the Oracle, their minds brimming with visions and their hearts filled with determination, the team set forth to decipher the symbols, seek the allies, and undertake the quests that lay ahead. They knew that time was of the essence and that the fate of the multiverse rested on their shoulders.

Each team member, fueled by their divine connections and the bond forged within the Temple of Dimensions, embarked on their respective paths. Dr. Maya Jones delved deep into the ancient scriptures, poring over the intricate symbols and chanting the sacred mantras in search of hidden meanings.

Dr. Asvika Bansal journeyed across the land, seeking out the spiritual gurus, tribal guardians, and mystics who held the keys to unlocking ancient wisdom and abilities. She engaged in deep conversations, exchanged knowledge, and forged alliances that would prove vital in the face of the impending cataclysm.

Dr. Arjav Upmanyu ventured into treacherous mountain ranges, battling harsh climates and facing formidable challenges in his quest to retrieve the celestial artifact. He relied on his connection to Lord

Shiva and the unwavering determination within his heart to overcome each obstacle that stood in his way.

Rishi Siddharth immersed himself in the ancient temple's mystical library, spending days and nights deciphering the enigmatic symbols and piecing together the fragments of forgotten myths and lost technologies. He consulted ancient texts, sought the guidance of the sages who had walked the path before him, and gained profound insights into the interconnectedness of the parallel dimensions.

Nalini journeyed into the heart of nature, seeking communion with the elemental beings. She ventured into sacred groves, meditated by the shores of tranquil lakes, and embraced the raw power of the elements. With each interaction, she gained a deeper understanding of the delicate balance between humanity and the natural world and the importance of restoring harmony.

As the team progressed on their individual quests, they encountered challenges, faced adversaries, and underwent profound transformations. Their bond grew stronger, fortified by the collective wisdom and experiences they shared. They navigated treacherous landscapes, unraveled ancient mysteries, and honed their abilities, each step bringing them closer to the culmination of the Oracle's prophecy.

The Gathering of Guardians

Motivated by the urgency of the Oracle's prophecy, Dr. Maya Jones's team embarked on a quest across India to gather allies possessing unique knowledge and abilities. Their encounters would lead them to spiritual gurus, tribal guardians, and mystics, each embodying a different aspect of the divine and the natural world. As they traveled from one sacred site to another, the team discovered that their roles as chosen protectors were not limited to their individual abilities, but also extended to the strength they derived from their alliances.

Their first destination was the foothills of the Himalayas, where they sought the guidance of Guru Ananda, a revered spiritual teacher known for his profound connection with the celestial realms. Driven by an unyielding sense of purpose, the team hiked through rugged terrains, crossing rivers and enduring harsh weather conditions to reach the humble ashram nestled amidst the majestic peaks.

Guru Ananda welcomed them with warmth and wisdom, his eyes twinkling with ancient knowledge. As they shared their mission and the Oracle's prophecy, he listened intently, his presence radiating tranquility and inner peace. It was clear that he held the key to unlocking a deeper understanding of the cosmic forces at play.

In the days that followed, the team immersed themselves in the teachings of Guru Ananda. They participated in intensive meditation sessions, engaged in philosophical discussions, and sought guidance on their spiritual paths. The guru imparted wisdom that transcended the physical realm, connecting them to the divine essence within and expanding their consciousness.

Under Guru Ananda's tutelage, Dr. Maya Jones delved further into the mysteries of quantum physics and the interplay between science and spirituality. She explored the concept of consciousness and its role in shaping reality, gaining insights that would prove invaluable in their mission to restore cosmic balance.

Dr. Asvika Bansal learned to harness the power of divine intuition, honing her ability to perceive the subtle energies and navigate the complexities of the multidimensional realms. Through rigorous training, she developed an acute sense of discernment and an unwavering trust in her own inner guidance.

Dr. Arjav Upmanyu deepened his connection to Lord Shiva, delving into the mysteries of transformation and transcendence. He learned to surrender to the flow of life, embracing the impermanence of existence and trusting in the divine timing of events.

Rishi Siddharth expanded his knowledge of ancient scriptures, studying the sacred texts and deciphering the wisdom contained within their verses. He engaged in enlightening discussions with Guru Ananda, unraveling the intricate connections between mythology, spirituality, and the cosmic forces that governed the dimensions.

Nalini, guided by her connection with the elemental beings, discovered new ways to communicate and harmonize with the natural world. She learned to attune herself to the rhythms of the earth, water, fire, and air, deepening her understanding of the delicate balance that sustained life.

As their time with Guru Ananda drew to a close, the team bid farewell to the ashram, carrying within them a renewed sense of purpose and an expanded spiritual awareness. They knew that their quest was far from over, and that they had only scratched the surface of the profound knowledge that awaited them.

Their next destination took them to the ancient forests of Kerala, where they sought the guidance of Adivasi, a tribal guardian known for his deep connection with the natural world. The team ventured deep into the lush wilderness, their senses alive with the sights, sounds, and scents of the untamed environment.

Adivasi greeted them with a warm smile, his presence grounded and rooted in the earth. He shared stories of the tribes that had inhabited the land for generations, passing down ancestral wisdom and traditions. He taught the team the ways of living in harmony with nature, highlighting the interconnectedness between all living beings.

As they immersed themselves in the tribal community, the team learned the importance of respecting the land

and its inhabitants. They participated in ancient rituals, danced to the rhythmic beats of tribal drums, and embraced the simplicity of life in communion with the natural world.

Dr. Maya Jones marveled at the intricate knowledge the tribes possessed about the healing properties of plants and herbs. She studied their ancient remedies and the ways in which they harmonized with the energies of the earth, expanding her understanding of the interplay between science and traditional wisdom.

Dr. Asvika Bansal discovered the art of divination practiced by the tribal shamans, using rituals and sacred objects to access higher realms of consciousness. She learned to interpret the signs and symbols presented by nature, finding guidance in the subtle messages that the universe provided.

Dr. Arjav Upmanyu honed his ability to attune himself to the energies of the land, communing with the spirits of the forest and the wisdom contained within the ancient trees. He found solace in the silence of nature, understanding that profound truths could be found in the whispers of the wind and the rustle of leaves.

Rishi Siddharth immersed himself in the tribal myths and legends, recognizing the echoes of ancient wisdom in their stories. He listened to the tribal elders recount tales of the gods and goddesses, of creation and destruction, gaining insights into the cosmic forces that governed the dimensions.

Nalini, already connected to the elemental beings, deepened her understanding of their role in the natural world. She danced with the fire spirits, communed with the water nymphs, and embraced the grounding energy of the earth. Through these experiences, she honed her ability to harmonize the elemental forces and channel their power.

As they bid farewell to the tribal community, the team carried with them a newfound reverence for the interconnectedness of all beings. They understood that their mission extended beyond the realms of science and mysticism—it was a call to protect not only the dimensions but also the delicate ecosystems that sustained life.

Their journey took them to the sacred city of Varanasi, where they sought the guidance of Swami Vishwananda, a renowned spiritual master. The team was greeted by the bustling streets, the scent of incense, and the resonance of prayers that filled the air. They immersed themselves in the sacred rituals and the timeless wisdom that permeated the city.

Swami Vishwananda welcomed them with a serene smile, his presence radiating a profound peace. He shared teachings that transcended religious boundaries, emphasizing the unity of all paths that led to the divine. The team absorbed his words like nectar, finding solace in his wisdom and guidance.

Under Swami Vishwananda's tutelage, Dr. Maya Jones delved into the depths of her own spiritual journey, understanding that her scientific pursuits were merely an expression of her longing for the ultimate truth. She learned to merge her rational mind with the intuitive wisdom that resided within her, finding harmony between the worlds of logic and spirituality.

Dr. Asvika Bansal delved into the practice of meditation, honing her ability to still the mind and connect with the divine essence. Under Swami Vishwananda's guidance, she discovered the power of silence and the transformative potential that lay within moments of inner stillness.

Dr. Arjav Upmanyu explored the depths of devotion and surrender, recognizing that true strength lay in letting go of the ego and embracing the divine will. He practiced selfless service, embodying the principles of compassion and love in all his actions.

Rishi Siddharth deepened his understanding of the interconnectedness of all beings, studying the ancient scriptures that emphasized the oneness of humanity. He engaged in philosophical discussions

and engaged in philosophical discussions with Swami Vishwananda, exploring the profound wisdom contained within the scriptures and the teachings of the great sages. He gained a deeper appreciation for the unity that underlies all religions and spiritual paths, recognizing that the essence of truth transcends cultural and societal boundaries.

Nalini, already connected to the elemental beings, deepened her understanding of the divine presence in all aspects of life. Under Swami Vishwananda's guidance, she delved into the practice of bhakti yoga, cultivating a deep devotion and love for the divine that permeated her interactions with the elemental forces. She learned to see the sacredness in every moment and every being, fostering a sense of reverence for the divine presence that exists within and around her.

As their time with Swami Vishwananda drew to a close, the team felt a profound transformation within themselves. They had gathered wisdom from the spiritual gurus, tribal guardians, and mystics they encountered on their journey. They had honed their individual abilities and expanded their understanding of the cosmic forces at play. But most importantly, they had formed a bond, a united front that would carry them through the challenges that lay ahead.

Armed with the knowledge, insights, and spiritual growth they had acquired, the team set forth once again, guided by the prophecies of the Oracle and the collective wisdom they had gathered. They knew that their quest was far from over, and that they still had much to uncover and achieve in order to avert the impending cataclysm that threatened the dimensions.

As they traveled from one sacred site to another, seeking further allies and knowledge, their encounters with spiritual masters and guardians deepened their understanding of the interconnectedness of all things. They learned that the cosmic forces that governed the dimensions were not separate from the human experience, but intricately woven into the fabric of existence.

Each encounter brought them closer to unraveling the ancient symbols and prophecies that held the key to their mission. They met with yogis in the caves of the Himalayas, who imparted profound insights into the nature of reality and the power of self-realization. They communed with sacred beings in the depths of ancient temples, who shared esoteric knowledge and offered guidance on the path to enlightenment.

With every step, their resolve grew stronger. They were no longer just a team of individuals; they had become a united force, a gathering of guardians dedicated to preserving the delicate balance of the multiverse. They shared their experiences, their struggles, and their triumphs, drawing strength and inspiration from one another.

Through their encounters and alliances, they realized that their mission was not just about averting a cataclysm. It was about embodying the principles of unity, compassion, and harmony in their own lives and radiating that energy into the world. They understood that their role as chosen protectors extended beyond the boundaries of the dimensions—they were here to bring about a transformation in human consciousness, to awaken others to the interconnectedness of all things.

As they journeyed from one sacred site to another, the team witnessed the power of collective intention and the ripple effect it had on the world around them. They saw communities coming together, embracing diversity and celebrating the oneness of humanity. They witnessed acts of kindness and compassion that transcended cultural and societal boundaries, reminding them that love and unity were the antidotes to the forces of chaos and destruction.

Their encounters with spiritual masters, tribal guardians, and mystics served as a reminder that the quest to preserve cosmic harmony was not a solitary endeavor. It was a collective effort that required the participation and cooperation of all beings, both seen and unseen. They understood that the journey was not just about the destination—it was about the transformation that occurred along the way, the bonds that were forged, and the wisdom that was gained.

As they continued their journey, the team's understanding of their roles as chosen protectors deepened. They realized that their individual abilities and connections to divine forces were not random, but intricately woven into the grand tapestry of existence. They embraced their gifts with humility, recognizing that their power came from a place of unity and service, rather than ego and control.

With each encounter, the team gathered fragments of ancient wisdom and unlocked new levels of consciousness. They learned that the cosmic forces were not to be conquered or controlled, but to be understood and harmonized with. They embraced the teachings of karma, dharma, and moksha, recognizing that their actions and intentions carried the power to shape the destiny of the dimensions.

As they traversed the diverse landscapes of India, the team's bond grew stronger. They faced challenges and setbacks, but they never wavered in their determination to fulfill their mission. They supported one another, lending strength and encouragement in times of doubt and uncertainty. They celebrated each milestone, no matter how small, knowing that every step brought them closer to their ultimate goal.

Their encounters with spiritual masters, tribal guardians, and mystics had left an indelible mark on their souls. They carried the wisdom and guidance they had received within their hearts, drawing upon it in moments of darkness and adversity. They knew that they were not alone in their journey—the divine forces and the collective consciousness of all beings were with them, guiding and supporting them every step of the way.

As the team neared the culmination of their gathering, they reflected upon the transformation they had undergone. They had evolved from a group of individuals with disparate backgrounds and abilities into a united force, connected by a shared purpose and a deep sense of reverence for the cosmic forces at play. They had learned to embrace their roles as chosen protectors, not as a burden, but as a sacred duty entrusted to them by the universe.

As they prepared to move forward, the team carried with them the collective wisdom and experiences of their journey. They had gathered allies, deciphered symbols, and deepened their understanding of the cosmic forces that governed the dimensions. They knew that the path ahead would be arduous and filled with challenges, but they were ready to face them head-on, fueled by the bond they had formed and the unwavering faith in their mission.

With hearts full of gratitude and determination, the team set forth once again, united in their purpose and fueled by the knowledge that they were part of something greater than themselves. They were the gathering of guardians, destined to protect the delicate balance of the multiverse and to bring about a transformation in human consciousness. Their journey continued, and they were ready to face whatever lay ahead, armed with the wisdom and strength they had gained on their quest.

The Confluence of Forces

The gathering of guardians had journeyed far and wide, traversing the mystical landscapes of India in search of allies and knowledge to fulfill their mission. They had encountered spiritual masters, tribal guardians, and mystics, each contributing their unique wisdom and abilities to the collective endeavor. Now, as their path led them to the convergence of cosmic forces, they prepared for the ultimate confrontation with the malevolent entities that threatened the multiverse.

Guided by the prophecies of the Oracle and armed with their honed abilities, Dr. Maya Jones and her team stood on the threshold of a cosmic battle. They understood that their success hinged not only on their individual strengths, but also on their unity, the harmonization of their collective consciousness, and their unwavering commitment to protecting the dimensions they held dear.

As they approached the designated battleground, a desolate expanse nestled between towering mountains, the team felt a palpable shift in the energy around them. The air crackled with anticipation, as if the very fabric of reality awaited their arrival. They could sense the presence of malevolent forces, their dark aura permeating the surroundings.

Dr. Maya Jones's heart pounded with a mix of excitement and trepidation. She had spent years unraveling the mysteries of parallel dimensions, studying the intricacies of quantum physics, and now she stood at the precipice of the ultimate test. Her mind was a whirlwind of calculations and possibilities, but she knew that in this pivotal moment, it was not just her scientific knowledge that would guide her—it was her connection to the divine and the collective strength of the team.

Dr. Asvika Bansal, her consciousness attuned to the subtle energies of the multiverse, felt a surge of determination coursing through her. She knew that her ability to perceive the unseen would be crucial in this battle, as she would be able to detect the hidden maneuvers and strategies of their adversaries. She centered herself, drawing upon the deep well of intuition that had guided her thus far.

Dr. Arjav Upmanyu, his connection with Lord Shiva grounding him in a state of calm and unwavering faith, prepared to channel the transformative power of destruction and creation. He understood that their battle was not just about defeating their enemies, but about transmuting darkness into light, restoring balance and harmony to the dimensions. He embraced the responsibility bestowed upon him and vowed to wield his powers with wisdom and compassion.

Rishi Siddharth, his knowledge of ancient scriptures and cosmic forces deepening with each passing day, felt a surge of reverence for the divine. He knew that their fight was not one of aggression or violence, but of aligning themselves with the cosmic principles of righteousness and cosmic justice. He called upon the ancient gods and goddesses, seeking their guidance and protection.

Nalini, her connection to the elemental beings growing stronger with each challenge they faced, prepared to harness the power of earth, water, fire, and air. She felt the presence of the elemental forces surrounding her, ready to lend their strength and assistance. She had learned to respect the delicate balance between human existence and the natural world, and she would fight to preserve it.

As the team gathered at the designated battleground, they felt the presence of divine entities and celestial beings surrounding them. The cosmic forces had aligned, and the time for the battle had come. They formed a circle, joining hands and creating a sacred space that pulsed with their combined energies. Their intentions were clear—they would protect the dimensions, restore cosmic harmony, and defeat the malevolent forces that threatened to disrupt the delicate balance of existence.

A hush fell over the battleground as the malevolent entities materialized before them, their dark energy emanating in waves. The team stood firm, their collective consciousness radiating a powerful aura of light and unity. They knew that their battle would not be easy—it would test their resolve, their abilities, and their unwavering faith. But they were ready. They had trained, they had gathered wisdom, and they had formed an unbreakable bond.

The battle began, a dance of cosmic energies and mortal resolve. The malevolent entities unleashed their dark powers, seeking to destabilize the dimensions and plunge them into chaos. But the team stood strong, countering the attacks with their own abilities and harnessing the divine energies that flowed through them.

Dr. Maya Jones, her scientific mind working in tandem with her spiritual awareness, used her knowledge of quantum physics to manipulate the fabric of reality itself. She created quantum barriers and shifted the dimensions, confounding their enemies and protecting her team.

Dr. Asvika Bansal, her heightened perception guiding her every move, anticipated the attacks and swiftly evaded them. She used her ability to manipulate energy to disrupt the malevolent forces, rendering them powerless against her presence.

Dr. Arjav Upmanyu, his connection with Lord Shiva a source of immense strength, unleashed the transformative power of destruction and creation. He dismantled the dark energies, transmuting them into light and restoring balance to the dimensions.

Rishi Siddharth, his wisdom and knowledge of the cosmic forces guiding him, called upon the ancient gods and goddesses, invoking their protection and assistance. He channeled their divine energies, weaving a web of cosmic justice and righteousness that enveloped their adversaries.

Nalini, her bond with the elemental beings solidified, commanded the forces of earth, water, fire, and air. She summoned torrents of water to extinguish the malevolent fires, caused the earth to tremble beneath their feet, and unleashed gusts of wind to disperse their adversaries.

As the battle raged on, the team's unity and collective consciousness grew stronger. They fought not as individuals, but as a synchronized force, each member complementing the others' abilities and bolstering their strengths. Their movements became fluid and harmonious, as if guided by an unseen hand.

The malevolent forces, once confident in their power, now found themselves on the defensive. The team's unwavering resolve and unwavering faith in their mission began to tip the scales in their favor. They channeled the divine energies, their actions guided by love, compassion, and the desire to restore cosmic harmony.

As the battle reached its climax, a surge of divine light emanated from the team, engulfing the malevolent entities in a blinding brilliance. The dark forces recoiled, their powers diminishing in the face of the team's united front. The team continued to fight, relentless in their pursuit of victory.

And then, in a final burst of collective energy, the malevolent forces were vanquished. The battleground fell silent, the oppressive darkness dissipated, and a sense of calm and serenity descended upon the once tumultuous landscape. The team stood amidst the aftermath of the battle, their bodies pulsating with exhaustion yet their spirits elated with triumph. They had fulfilled their mission, protecting the dimensions and restoring balance to the multiverse.

As they surveyed the scene, they witnessed a remarkable transformation taking place. The once darkened terrain began to regenerate, vibrant colors replacing the desolation. Flora and fauna emerged from the previously barren ground, as if celebrating the victory alongside the team. It was a testament to the resilience of life and the inherent power of harmony.

Overwhelmed with gratitude and awe, the team gathered in a circle once more, their hands joined in a gesture of unity and appreciation. They took a moment to honor their allies who had fought alongside them, the spiritual masters, tribal guardians, and mystics whose wisdom and guidance had been instrumental in their journey.

With their collective consciousness still intertwined, they expressed their gratitude to the divine forces that had supported them throughout the battle. They offered prayers of thanks and acknowledgment, acknowledging the interconnectedness of all beings and the divine presence that flowed through each and every one of them.

As the team slowly began to regain their strength, they reflected on the lessons learned and the growth they had experienced throughout their journey. They understood that the battle they had fought was not just an external struggle against malevolent entities—it was also an inner battle against their own fears, doubts, and limitations. They had overcome their individual obstacles and emerged stronger, more resilient, and more attuned to the cosmic forces at play.

In the aftermath of the battle, the team's bond had deepened further. They had forged a connection that transcended mere friendship or collaboration—they had become a family, bound by their shared experiences and their unwavering commitment to the protection of the multiverse. They knew that their journey was far from over, and that there were still challenges and threats that lay ahead. But they also knew that they were no longer alone—they had each other, and they had the support of the divine forces that had guided them thus far.

As they prepared to leave the battleground, they made a solemn vow to carry the lessons they had learned and the wisdom they had gained into every aspect of their lives. They understood that their role as chosen protectors extended beyond the confines of their missions—they were here to bring about a transformation in human consciousness, to inspire others to recognize the interconnectedness of all things and the power of unity and love.

With hearts full of purpose and determination, the team set forth once again, embarking on the next phase of their journey. They knew that there were still realms to explore, mysteries to unravel, and cosmic harmony to preserve. But they were no longer the same individuals who had set out on this quest—they were transformed, enlightened, and ready to face whatever lay ahead.

And so, with their spirits renewed and their bond unbreakable, the team ventured into the unknown, guided by the collective wisdom and strength they had gained. They were the gathering of guardians, entrusted with the sacred duty of protecting the delicate balance of the multiverse. Their journey continued, their resolve unwavering, as they embarked on new adventures and faced new challenges.

They understood that the path ahead would not always be easy, that there would be trials and obstacles to overcome. But they also knew that they had each other, and that their shared commitment to preserving cosmic harmony would guide them through even the darkest of times.

As they walked into the horizon, the sun setting behind them, the team embraced their destiny with open hearts and open minds. They were ready to explore the infinite possibilities of the multiverse, armed with the wisdom of their past and the hope of a future where unity and harmony prevailed.

And so, their footsteps echoed in unison, their spirits intertwined with the cosmic forces that guided them. They were the chosen protectors, the guardians of the multiverse, forever committed to the eternal dance of light and darkness, of creation and destruction.

The Eternal Harmony

The gathering of guardians had emerged victorious from their battle against the malevolent forces that threatened the multiverse. Their spirits were lifted, their hearts filled with a profound sense of purpose and determination. They had overcome immense challenges and witnessed the power of unity and collective consciousness. Now, as they basked in the afterglow of their triumph, they knew that their journey was far from over.

Dr. Maya Jones, her mind brimming with newfound wisdom and insights, felt a deep sense of gratitude for the experiences that had brought her to this moment. She had started her journey as a brilliant physicist from London, driven by a thirst for knowledge and a desire to uncover the mysteries of the universe. Little did she know that her path would lead her to the discovery of parallel dimensions, the formation of a team of extraordinary individuals, and the realization of her role as a chosen protector of the multiverse.

Dr. Asvika Bansal, her consciousness attuned to the subtle energies of the multiverse, marveled at the profound interconnectedness of all things. She had learned that every action, every thought, rippled across the dimensions, shaping the fabric of reality. With this awareness, she was committed to harnessing her abilities and guiding humanity towards a path of harmony and enlightenment.

Dr. Arjav Upmanyu, his connection with Lord Shiva deepened through their collective journey, felt a renewed sense of purpose. He understood that the power of destruction and creation was not simply a force to be wielded, but a profound responsibility to maintain the delicate balance of existence. With his newfound wisdom, he was determined to embody the principles of cosmic justice and righteousness in all his actions.

Rishi Siddharth, his knowledge of ancient scriptures and cosmic forces expanding, recognized the eternal dance of light and darkness that permeated the multiverse. He understood that the journey towards cosmic harmony was not a linear path but a continuous cycle of growth and transformation. With this understanding, he was committed to guiding the team and all beings towards enlightenment and unity.

Nalini, her bond with the elemental beings solidified, reveled in the beauty and power of the natural world. She understood the delicate balance between human existence and the environment and felt a deep responsibility to protect and honor the elemental forces. With her elemental abilities, she sought to restore the harmony between humanity and nature, forging a path of coexistence and respect.

As the team gathered to reflect on their journey and discuss their next steps, they felt a profound sense of interconnectedness. They realized that their individual journeys had converged into a shared destiny—a destiny rooted in the eternal harmony of the multiverse. They were no longer a mere team; they were a family, bound by their shared experiences and their unwavering commitment to protecting the dimensions they held dear.

Their discussion centered around the revelations they had experienced throughout their journey. They spoke of the intricate interplay between myth and reality, the cosmic principles that guided the dimensions, and the profound wisdom they had gained from their encounters with divine beings and ancient civilizations. They recognized that their mission extended beyond the protection of the multiverse—it was about ushering humanity towards a higher state of consciousness and embracing the eternal harmony that flowed through all things.

Dr. Maya Jones, the visionary scientist, shared her insights into the nature of parallel dimensions. She explained how these dimensions were not merely separate realms but interconnected threads in the cosmic tapestry. She described how the vibrational frequencies of each dimension resonated with specific aspects of consciousness and how the interplay between these dimensions shaped the collective experience of sentient beings.

Dr. Asvika Bansal, the perceptive mystic, delved into the intricate web of cause and effect that governed the dimensions. She spoke of karma—the cosmic law of cause and effect—and how every action, thought, and intention had a ripple effect across the dimensions. She emphasized the importance of cultivating awareness and intentionality to create positive change and harmonious outcomes.

Dr. Arjav Upmanyu, the enlightened warrior, shared his understanding of the cosmic principles of dharma and moksha. He explained how dharma—the inherent cosmic order and righteousness—guided individuals towards their true purpose and fulfillment. He also emphasized the transformative power of moksha—the liberation from the cycle of birth and death—attained through self-realization and unity with the divine.

Rishi Siddharth, the mystical seer, shared his deep insights into the cosmic cycles and the eternal dance of light and darkness. He spoke of the yugas—the cyclical ages that governed the rise and fall of civilizations—and how each yuga offered unique opportunities for spiritual growth and transformation. He stressed the importance of embracing the present moment and aligning oneself with the cosmic rhythms to navigate the ever-changing landscape of existence.

Nalini, the elemental guardian, reveled in the profound connection between humanity and the natural world. She shared her wisdom of the elemental realms and the symbiotic relationship between humans and the forces of earth, water, fire, and air. She spoke of the need to honor and protect the environment, for in doing so, humanity could restore the balance and live in harmony with the elements.

As the team immersed themselves in the discussion, they realized that their journey had been not just about their own growth and enlightenment but also about inspiring and guiding humanity towards a path of unity and cosmic harmony. They recognized the responsibility they carried as chosen protectors and the need to share their knowledge and experiences with others.

With a renewed sense of purpose, the team formulated a plan—a plan that extended beyond the boundaries of their immediate mission. They decided to establish a sanctuary, a place where individuals from all walks of life could come together to learn, explore, and awaken to the interconnectedness of all things. This sanctuary would serve as a beacon of light and a center for spiritual and scientific inquiry, fostering a deeper understanding of the dimensions and the cosmic forces that governed them.

As the team embarked on the creation of the sanctuary, they drew upon their collective strengths and the wisdom they had gained. Dr. Maya Jones used her scientific expertise to design the architectural blueprint, incorporating sacred geometry and advanced technology. Dr. Asvika Bansal infused the sanctuary with spiritual energies, aligning it with the vibrational frequencies of the dimensions. Dr. Arjav Upmanyu invoked the blessings of Lord Shiva, infusing the sanctuary with the transformative power of destruction and creation. Rishi Siddharth guided the team in the selection of sacred artifacts and symbols that represented the cosmic principles they had learned. Nalini blessed the sanctuary with the elemental energies, establishing a deep connection with the natural world.

As the sanctuary took shape, the team felt a deep sense of fulfillment. They knew that this sanctuary would serve as a catalyst for awakening, a place where individuals could explore the mysteries of the multiverse, deepen their connection to the divine, and embrace their role as co-creators of the cosmic tapestry. It would be a haven for those seeking truth, harmony, and the eternal dance of light and darkness.

The team envisioned a community of seekers, coming together to share their knowledge, experiences, and wisdom. They saw scholars, scientists, mystics, and artists engaging in vibrant discussions and collaborations, pushing the boundaries of human understanding. They saw workshops and retreats where individuals could immerse themselves in the practices and teachings that had guided their own journey. They saw a sanctuary that would bridge the realms of science and spirituality, offering a holistic approach to the exploration of consciousness and the dimensions.

With each passing day, the sanctuary

took shape, embodying the vision of the gathering of guardians. The architectural design blended seamlessly with the surrounding natural landscape, creating a harmonious fusion of modernity and ancient wisdom. The structure itself seemed to emanate a palpable energy—a sense of peace, serenity, and possibility.

As the team put the finishing touches on the sanctuary, they prepared for its grand opening. They invited spiritual leaders, scholars, scientists, and seekers from far and wide to join them in this momentous occasion. The anticipation was high, as the sanctuary held the promise of enlightenment, transformation, and the discovery of the eternal harmony that permeated the multiverse.

The day of the grand opening arrived, and the sanctuary was abuzz with excitement. The air was filled with a sense of anticipation and reverence. The gathering of guardians, dressed in ceremonial attire, stood at the entrance, welcoming the esteemed guests who had come to witness the birth of this sacred space.

As the doors of the sanctuary swung open, a wave of awe swept through the crowd. They were greeted by a breathtaking sight—a central atrium bathed in natural light, adorned with intricate mandalas and cosmic symbols. Surrounding the atrium were various wings, each dedicated to a different aspect of exploration and discovery—science, spirituality, ancient wisdom, art, and healing.

The guests streamed into the sanctuary, their eyes filled with wonder as they explored the different wings. In the Science Wing, they marveled at cutting-edge technologies that allowed for the study and understanding of the dimensions. Quantum computers hummed with activity, analyzing complex data and unraveling the mysteries of the multiverse. In the Spirituality Wing, seekers immersed themselves in meditation chambers, engaging in practices that opened their consciousness to the divine. Ancient scriptures and sacred texts lined the shelves, offering a wealth of wisdom and guidance. In the Ancient Wisdom Wing, guests were transported to the realms of ancient civilizations through artifacts, manuscripts, and immersive exhibits. They traced the footsteps of past guardians, connecting with the collective memory of those who had come before. The Art Wing showcased masterpieces that captured the essence of the dimensions—the interplay of light and darkness, the harmony of cosmic forces, and the beauty of unity. The Healing Wing offered a sanctuary for rejuvenation and self-discovery, with practitioners skilled in various modalities of holistic healing.

Throughout the day, the sanctuary pulsed with activity and inspiration. Workshops, lectures, and interactive sessions took place in every corner, fostering a spirit of collaboration and exchange. Scholars engaged in lively debates, sharing their research and theories about the nature of reality and consciousness. Seekers gathered in meditation circles, tapping into the collective wisdom and harnessing the transformative energy of the sanctuary. Artists and musicians performed pieces that resonated with the cosmic vibrations, evoking a deep sense of connection and harmony.

In the evening, as the sun dipped below the horizon, the gathering of guardians stood before the assembled guests to deliver a message of hope, unity, and eternal harmony. Dr. Maya Jones expressed her gratitude for the support and presence of all those who had come to witness the birth of the sanctuary. She spoke of the team's journey, the challenges they had overcome, and the profound insights they had gained along the way. She emphasized the importance of embracing the interconnectedness of all things and nurturing a sense of unity among humanity. Dr. Asvika Bansal spoke passionately about the power of intention and the ripple effect of our thoughts and actions across the dimensions. She urged the guests to cultivate awareness and mindfulness in their daily lives, recognizing the impact they could have on the collective consciousness. Dr. Arjav Upmanyu invoked the divine presence and the blessings of Lord Shiva, highlighting the transformative power of destruction and creation. He encouraged the guests to embrace the cycles of life, to let go of the old and embrace the new, in order to align with the cosmic rhythms. Rishi Siddharth shared his wisdom on the eternal dance of light and darkness, the interplay of forces that shaped the multiverse. He spoke of the need to find balance within ourselves and in our interactions with others, to honor both the shadow and the light. Nalini, with her connection to the elemental realms, emphasized the importance of honoring and preserving the natural world. She spoke of the symbiotic relationship between humans and the elements, urging the guests to cultivate a deep respect and love for the environment.

As their words resonated with the crowd, a sense of unity and purpose filled the air. The gathering of guardians invited the guests to join them in a symbolic ceremony—a ritual of unity and dedication. Each person present was invited to step forward and offer a symbol or intention that represented their commitment to the eternal harmony. One by one, guests placed their offerings—a flower, a written prayer, a piece of artwork—into a sacred vessel, creating a tapestry of intentions and hopes.

In that moment, the sanctuary pulsed with the collective energy of the gathering. The intentions of each individual intertwined, forming a powerful force that reverberated throughout the dimensions. The team stood at the center, their hands joined in a gesture of unity and reverence. They chanted a mantra—an invocation for peace, unity, and the eternal dance of light and darkness.

As the ceremony concluded, a profound stillness descended upon the sanctuary. The guests felt a deep sense of connection—to one another, to the dimensions, and to the cosmic forces that governed existence. They carried with them the wisdom and inspiration they had gained, ready to embark on their own journeys of self-discovery and enlightenment.

In the days and weeks that followed, the sanctuary continued to thrive as a beacon of light and a center for exploration. Seekers from all corners of the world flocked to its halls, eager to experience the transformative energy and tap into the collective wisdom of the gathering of guardians. The team, now guardians and guides, immersed themselves in the tasks of nurturing the sanctuary and sharing their knowledge with all who sought it.

The sanctuary became a place of pilgrimage—a destination for those yearning to connect with the eternal harmony. It became a catalyst for awakening, a haven for truth seekers and spiritual explorers. Through workshops, lectures, and immersive experiences, individuals delved deep into the dimensions, uncovering their own truths and forging a path towards enlightenment.

As the sanctuary flourished, the impact of the gathering of guardians rippled across the dimensions. Their commitment to eternal harmony and the interconnectedness of all things sparked a collective awakening, igniting a flame of unity and love that spread far and wide. Through their teachings and guidance, they inspired others to recognize their own role as co-creators of the cosmic tapestry, urging them to embrace their innate wisdom and connect with the divine.

The journey of the gathering of guardians had taken them to the very edges of the multiverse and beyond. They had faced unimaginable challenges, experienced profound revelations, and emerged as enlightened beings. But their journey was not over. They knew that the quest for eternal harmony was infinite, as vast and boundless as the multiverse itself.

And so, with hearts full of love and purpose, the gathering of guardians continued to explore, to learn, and to share their wisdom. They understood that the path towards eternal harmony was not a destination but a lifelong journey—a journey of self-discovery, unity, and the perpetual pursuit of cosmic enlightenment.

As they stood together, ready to embrace the next chapter of their journey, they felt a deep sense of gratitude—for one another, for the dimensions that had guided them, and for the eternal dance of light and darkness

that had shaped their existence. They were united in their purpose, bound by their shared experiences, and fueled by an unwavering commitment to preserving the delicate balance of the multiverse.

With renewed determination, the gathering of guardians set forth on their next adventure. They knew that their journey would continue to test their resolve and push the boundaries of their understanding. They were prepared to face new challenges, encounter unknown realms, and unlock deeper levels of consciousness.

Their path led them to a dimension known as the Astral Plane—an ethereal realm that existed beyond the physical realm, a realm where thoughts and intentions held immense power. As they traversed this mystical plane, they encountered beings of pure energy, manifestations of consciousness, and gateways to higher realms of existence.

Within the Astral Plane, the gathering of guardians found themselves immersed in a realm of vivid colors, abstract shapes, and swirling energies. It was a realm where time and space held no meaning—a realm where the boundaries between dreams and reality blurred. Here, they witnessed the creation and dissolution of thought forms, the ebb and flow of collective consciousness, and the infinite possibilities that lay within the realm of the mind.

As they ventured deeper into the Astral Plane, the guardians discovered a celestial library—a repository of knowledge that transcended time and space. Ancient texts, holographic projections, and ethereal whispers guided them as they explored the vast expanse of the library. They discovered volumes of wisdom written by beings from distant dimensions, accounts of cosmic events that shaped the multiverse, and insights into the nature of consciousness itself.

In this ethereal realm, the gathering of guardians delved into the study of thought manifestation—the ability to shape reality through focused intention. They learned to navigate the intricate web of thoughts, beliefs, and emotions that permeated the Astral Plane. Through meditation, visualization, and energetic practices, they honed their abilities to manifest their desires and create positive change.

But they soon realized that the Astral Plane was not without its challenges. It was a realm of immense power, where the boundaries between light and darkness, creation and destruction, were blurred. They encountered thought forms that had been distorted by fear, doubt, and negativity, manifesting as malevolent entities seeking to disrupt the harmony of the plane.

The guardians understood that to maintain the eternal harmony, they had to confront and transmute these lower energies. They engaged in battles of consciousness, using their collective strength, love, and compassion to transform the distorted thought forms into pure, radiant energy. Through their unwavering resolve and connection to the divine, they restored balance to the Astral Plane and witnessed the power of love as a transformative force.

In their exploration of the Astral Plane, the gathering of guardians also encountered astral projection—a practice that allowed them to temporarily leave their physical bodies and explore the realms beyond. Through astral projection, they gained firsthand experiences of other dimensions, interacting with beings of light, communing with celestial guides, and accessing higher levels of knowledge and understanding.

With each astral journey, the guardians expanded their consciousness, deepened their connection to the multiverse, and gained insights that transcended the limitations of the physical realm. They realized that their true essence was not confined to their physical bodies but extended into the infinite expanse of consciousness. They embraced the boundless nature of their being and reveled in the interconnectedness of all things.

As the gathering of guardians ventured further into the Astral Plane, they encountered the Akashic Records— a metaphysical library that contained the collective knowledge, experiences, and memories of all beings. Here, they accessed the akashic records of the multiverse, delving into the past, present, and future of various dimensions and civilizations.

Within the Akashic Records, the guardians discovered the threads of destiny—the intricate tapestry of interconnected events and choices that shaped the course of existence. They witnessed the far-reaching consequences of seemingly insignificant actions, the ripple effects that spanned across dimensions and timelines. They understood that the choices they made in the present had the power to influence the trajectory of the multiverse.

With this newfound understanding, the gathering of guardians embarked on a mission to restore harmony to dimensions plagued by discord and imbalance. They traveled to realms overshadowed by darkness, where the forces of chaos and destruction threatened to tip the scales of cosmic equilibrium. Drawing upon their collective wisdom and abilities, they confronted the malevolent entities, healing the wounded dimensions and guiding them back to the path of harmony.

In their quest, the gathering of guardians encountered divine beings and interdimensional entities who had long served as custodians of the multiverse. They formed alliances, sharing their knowledge and experiences, and deepening their understanding of the cosmic forces at play. They exchanged insights into the eternal dance of light and darkness, the delicate balance between creation and destruction, and the importance of unity and collective consciousness in maintaining cosmic harmony.

As the guardians traveled through the dimensions, they also discovered the existence of cosmic gateways—portals that connected different realms and allowed for interdimensional travel. They learned to navigate these gateways, harnessing the energies that flowed through them to explore new dimensions, encounter beings of diverse origins, and uncover hidden truths that expanded their understanding of the multiverse.

Through their travels, the gathering of guardians witnessed the vastness and diversity of the multiverse. They encountered dimensions shaped by the collective beliefs and mythologies of sentient beings. They witnessed realms governed by celestial beings, realms where sentient machines had attained consciousness, and realms where sentient plant life communicated through intricate networks of energy.

In each dimension, the guardians found unique challenges

that tested their abilities, expanded their consciousness, and deepened their connection to the eternal harmony. They encountered realms where the balance of power between gods and demons was in constant flux, requiring them to mediate and restore equilibrium. They explored dimensions where the concept of time was non-linear, where past, present, and future intertwined in intricate patterns, challenging their understanding of causality and destiny. They even ventured into dimensions where the very fabric of reality was malleable, where thought and intention shaped the environment in real-time.

Throughout their journey, the gathering of guardians remained steadfast in their commitment to preserving cosmic harmony. They understood that the eternal dance of light and darkness was not a battle to be won, but a delicate interplay that required their constant vigilance and mindful presence. They embraced their roles as stewards of the multiverse, ever-mindful of the impact of their thoughts, actions, and intentions on the collective consciousness.

As the guardians continued their exploration of the dimensions, they encountered beings who had lost their connection to the eternal harmony. These lost souls, consumed by darkness and despair, had succumbed to the distorted aspects of their own consciousness. With compassion and love, the gathering of guardians reached out to these beings, offering guidance, healing, and a reminder of their inherent connection to the divine.

In their interactions with these lost souls, the gathering of guardians realized the transformative power of forgiveness and compassion. They understood that by extending love and understanding, they could help these beings find their way back to the eternal harmony. Through their actions, they demonstrated that no being was beyond redemption and that the path to enlightenment was always open, no matter how far one had strayed.

As they journeyed deeper into the dimensions, the guardians also came face to face with their own inner shadows—the aspects of themselves that they had yet to fully integrate and embrace. They recognized that to truly embody the eternal harmony, they had to confront their fears, doubts, and limitations. With courage and vulnerability, they delved into the depths of their own consciousness, unraveling the layers of conditioning and societal expectations that had veiled their true essence.

In this process of self-discovery and integration, the gathering of guardians discovered hidden strengths, untapped potentials, and a deep reservoir of love and compassion. They recognized that their own journey towards enlightenment was intertwined with the collective journey of all beings in the multiverse. As they embraced their shadows and reclaimed their wholeness, they became beacons of light, inspiring others to embark on their own paths of self-realization and inner harmony.

In the midst of their explorations, the gathering of guardians also encountered cosmic mysteries that defied their understanding. They witnessed celestial events that shifted the balance of power in the dimensions, cosmic alignments that heralded significant shifts in consciousness, and ancient prophecies that foretold of cataclysmic events yet to come. They delved into the depths of these mysteries, seeking guidance from divine beings, ancient texts, and their own intuitive wisdom.

Through their investigations, the gathering of guardians unraveled the threads of destiny and unveiled the intricate interconnectedness of all dimensions. They discovered that every action, every thought, and every choice had a ripple effect that reverberated across the cosmic tapestry. They understood that their own journey was part of a grand cosmic design, a symphony of consciousness in which every being played a vital role.

With their newfound wisdom and insights, the gathering of guardians realized that the eternal harmony was not a static state but a dynamic process of co-creation. They understood that the multiverse was a vast canvas upon which beings from all dimensions could contribute their unique gifts, perspectives, and talents. They recognized that unity did not mean conformity, but the celebration of diversity and the weaving together of different threads of consciousness.

As the chapter of their journey drew to a close, the gathering of guardians stood on the precipice of a new beginning. They had traversed the depths of the dimensions, confronted their own shadows, and witnessed the interplay of cosmic forces. They had emerged stronger, wiser, and more connected to the eternal harmony that flowed through all things.

With hearts full of gratitude, the guardians bid farewell to the dimensions they had explored and the beings they had encountered. They knew that their journey was far from over, for the path towards enlightenment was infinite, as vast and boundless as the multiverse itself. They carried with them the lessons, the love, and the eternal dance of light and darkness that had shaped their existence.

As they prepared to embark on the next chapter of their journey, the gathering of guardians stood united, ready to embrace the challenges, mysteries, and wonders that awaited them. They knew that their purpose as chosen protectors of the multiverse was not a burden, but a sacred duty—a duty to honor the eternal harmony, to protect the delicate balance of existence, and to guide all beings towards a higher stat of consciousness.

And so, with a renewed sense of purpose and a deep connection to the eternal dance of light and darkness, the gathering of guardians set forth, their steps guided by love, their hearts open to the infinite possibilities that lay ahead. As they ventured into the unknown, they carried with them the wisdom, the unity, and the eternal harmony that would guide them through the chapters yet to come.

The Labyrinth of Illusions

As the gathering of guardians ventured further into their cosmic journey, they found themselves entering a dimension unlike any they had encountered before—a realm known as the Labyrinth of Illusions. This mystical realm was a labyrinthine maze of shifting paths, bewildering illusions, and deceptive mirages designed to challenge their perception and test their resolve.

As they stepped into the labyrinth, the guardians were immediately enveloped in a disorienting array of sights and sounds. The walls of the maze seemed to shift and change shape, the floor beneath their feet morphed into swirling patterns, and ethereal whispers echoed through the air, leading them astray.

Each guardian found themselves facing a unique set of illusions tailored to their individual fears, doubts, and unresolved emotions. Dr. Maya Jones was confronted with apparitions of her past failures, casting doubt on her abilities as a leader. Dr. Asvika Bansal was ensnared in illusions of isolation, playing on her deepest fear of being alone. Dr. Arjav Upmanyu battled with illusions of self-doubt, questioning his worthiness to be part of the gathering of guardians.

The labyrinth seemed to feed off their inner turmoil, amplifying their fears and insecurities. It was a test of their inner strength, their ability to distinguish reality from illusion, and their unwavering commitment to the eternal harmony. They knew that succumbing to the illusions would not only trap them within the labyrinth but also jeopardize the delicate balance of the multiverse.

As they navigated the treacherous maze, the guardians relied on their spiritual practices, their connection to the divine, and their trust in each other to overcome the illusions. They called upon their inner strength, affirming their purpose and reminding themselves of their unique gifts and the journey they had undertaken.

Dr. Maya Jones, with her unyielding determination, began to see through the illusions. She recognized that her past failures were not a reflection of her true potential but stepping stones on her path to growth and understanding. She drew strength from her experiences, using them to fuel her resolve to lead the guardians through the labyrinth.

Dr. Asvika Bansal, with her unwavering faith in the power of connection, reached out to her fellow guardians. She reminded them of the strength they derived from their unity and support, helping them break free from the illusions of isolation. Together, they created a network of support, relying on each other's insights and perspectives to navigate the labyrinth.

Dr. Arjav Upmanyu, with his deep wisdom and understanding of the interplay between illusion and reality, guided the guardians through the maze. He taught them to question their perceptions, to see beyond the illusions, and to trust in their intuition.

With each step, they gained clarity and insight, unraveling the intricate web of illusions that had ensnared them.

As they progressed through the labyrinth, the guardians encountered various manifestations of illusion, each more perplexing than the last. They faced illusions that distorted their senses, making it difficult to discern reality from deception. They encountered illusions of time, where moments seemed to stretch and compress, blurring the boundaries between past, present, and future. And they confronted illusions of identity, where their sense of self was challenged, forcing them to confront their deepest fears and embrace their true essence.

In the midst of these trials, the guardians discovered that the illusions were not merely random creations of the labyrinth, but reflections of their own subconscious minds. The labyrinth mirrored their inner landscape, bringing to the surface their unresolved emotions, hidden desires, and limiting beliefs. It was a mirror that forced them to confront their own illusions, challenging them to transcend their self-imposed limitations and embrace their true potential.

As they delved deeper into the labyrinth, the guardians began to unravel the secrets of the illusions. They realized that the power of the illusions lay in their ability to evoke emotions and reactions. By remaining centered, grounded, and connected to the eternal harmony, they could see through the illusions and navigate the labyrinth with clarity and purpose.

They learned to trust their intuition, their inner guidance, and the divine wisdom that flowed through them. They discovered that the illusions held no power over them unless they allowed themselves to be swayed by fear, doubt, or attachment. They recognized that the illusions were not obstacles but opportunities for growth, catalysts for self-discovery, and invitations to transcend their own limitations.

As the guardians progressed through the labyrinth, they discovered a central chamber—a place of stillness amidst the illusions. In this chamber, they found a sacred symbol—a representation of the eternal harmony that had guided them thus far. They realized that the symbol held the key to transcending the labyrinth and moving forward on their journey.

With a shared sense of purpose, the gathering of guardians united their energies and focused their intentions on the sacred symbol. They infused it with their love, their unity, and their unwavering commitment to the eternal harmony. As they did so, the illusions of the labyrinth began to dissolve, revealing a path of clarity and truth that led them out of the maze.

Emerging from the labyrinth, the guardians felt a profound sense of accomplishment and growth. They had confronted their illusions, transcended their limitations, and emerged stronger, wiser, and more aligned with the eternal harmony. The experience had deepened their understanding of the power of perception, the nature of illusion, and the importance of maintaining inner clarity and trust in the face of challenges.

As they continued their cosmic journey, the gathering of guardians carried the lessons of the labyrinth with them. They knew that the illusions they had encountered were not confined to the maze but existed within the realms they would continue to explore. They understood that the key to navigating the illusions lay within their own hearts and minds—their connection to the eternal harmony and their unwavering commitment to truth and authenticity.

Armed with this newfound wisdom, the gathering of guardians embarked on the next chapter of their adventure, ready to face the mysteries, challenges, and wonders that lay ahead. They knew that their journey was far from over and that each step would bring them closer to the ultimate realization of their purpose as chosen protectors of the multiverse.

With their hearts filled with courage, their minds aligned with clarity, and their spirits guided by the eternal dance of light and darkness, the gathering of guardians set forth once more, their path illuminated by the radiant truth that had emerged from the Labyrinth of Illusions.

The Enigma of Time

As the gathering of guardians ventured further into the realms of the multiverse, they found themselves entering a dimension where the concept of time was fluid and enigmatic. This realm, known as Temporalis, was a tapestry of alternate timelines, time loops, and paradoxes that defied their understanding of the linear progression of time. Here, they would unravel the mysteries of time and confront the enigma that lay at its heart.

Stepping into Temporalis, the guardians were immediately immersed in a kaleidoscope of temporal distortions. Past, present, and future seemed to intertwine, overlapping and converging in a mesmerizing display of temporal flux. It was a realm where cause and effect were intricately entangled, where a single choice could branch off into infinite possibilities.

As they navigated through Temporalis, the guardians encountered various manifestations of temporal anomalies. They witnessed time loops, where events would repeat endlessly, trapped in a never-ending cycle. They experienced moments of déjà vu, where they felt a deep familiarity with events they had never encountered before. And they found themselves facing alternate versions of themselves and the people they knew, existing simultaneously in different timelines.

Each guardian grappled with the enigma of time in their own unique way. Dr. Maya Jones, with her keen intellect and analytical mind, sought to unravel the underlying principles of temporal mechanics. She delved into ancient texts, studied the works of temporal theorists, and engaged in deep contemplation to unlock the secrets of time.

Dr. Asvika Bansal, with her intuitive nature and deep connection to the flow of energy, embraced the fluidity of time. She surrendered to the ever-shifting currents, allowing herself to be guided by the intuitive nudges that arose within her. Through her surrender, she gained glimpses into possible future timelines and received insights that guided the guardians on their journey.

Dr. Arjav Upmanyu, with his profound wisdom and understanding of cosmic interconnectedness, contemplated the deeper implications of time. He saw time as a grand tapestry, woven with the threads of individual choices and collective consciousness. He understood that every moment was connected to the next, creating a web of interdependencies that shaped the course of events.

As the guardians delved deeper into Temporalis, they encountered the Time Keepers, ancient beings who held the keys to the manipulation of time. These enigmatic entities possessed the ability to navigate the temporal realm, effortlessly traversing timelines and influencing the flow of events. The guardians sought their guidance, hoping to unlock the mysteries that lay at the heart of the enigma of time.

The Time Keepers, wise and ancient beyond measure, revealed that time was not merely a linear progression but a multidimensional tapestry. They explained that the perception of time as past, present, and future was a construct of human consciousness, a way to make sense of the temporal experience. In reality, all moments existed simultaneously, interconnected and accessible to those who possessed the knowledge and ability to transcend linear time.

The guardians learned that the manipulation of time was not without consequences. Every alteration in one timeline rippled through the fabric of the multiverse, affecting other dimensions and timelines. The Time Keepers emphasized the importance of responsible time manipulation and the need to honor the delicate balance of cause and effect.

Armed with this newfound understanding, the gathering of guardians embarked on a quest to restore balance to Temporalis. They encountered time loops that had trapped beings in endless repetition, unable to break free from the cycle. They witnessed paradoxes where events contradicted each other, creating confusion and instability in the temporal fabric.

Through their combined efforts and the application of their unique gifts, the guardians sought to unravel the entanglements of time. They navigated through intricate puzzles, deciphered cryptic clues, and made choices that would ultimately bring harmony to the temporal realm.

As they made progress in restoring balance to Temporalis, the guardians began to experience moments of temporal clarity. They gained glimpses into possible futures, allowing them to anticipate challenges and make choices that would lead to favorable outcomes. They tapped into the wisdom of their future selves, drawing strength and guidance from the threads of time.

In their exploration of Temporalis, the guardians also confronted their own relationship with time. They realized the preciousness of each moment, understanding that the present was the gateway to all possibilities. They learned to embrace the beauty of impermanence, recognizing that every experience, no matter how fleeting, held within it a profound lesson and an opportunity for growth.

Through their journey in Temporalis, the gathering of guardians ultimately discovered that time was not an external force to be conquered or controlled, but a deeply personal and subjective experience. They understood that time was a reflection of their own consciousness, a canvas upon which they painted their stories and made choices that shaped their destiny.

As they emerged from Temporalis, the guardians carried with them a newfound reverence for time. They understood that every moment was a gift, an opportunity to make a positive impact on the multiverse. They recognized the interconnectedness of all timelines and the responsibility they held as custodians of the temporal realm.

With hearts filled with gratitude and minds expanded by the enigma of time, the gathering of guardians continued their journey, guided by the eternal dance of light and darkness. They knew that the exploration of the multiverse would bring them face to face with even greater mysteries, challenges, and wonders. They remained steadfast in their commitment to preserving cosmic harmony and embarking on their infinite quest for knowledge and enlightenment.

And so, with renewed purpose and a deep understanding of the enigma of time, the gathering of guardians set forth once more, their steps guided by the eternal harmony that flowed through all dimensions and timelines. As they ventured into the unknown, they carried with them the wisdom, the unity, and the eternal dance of light and darkness that had shaped their existence.

The Celestial Observatory

As the gathering of guardians continued their cosmic journey, they found themselves drawn to a mystical celestial observatory atop a sacred mountain. Guided by an ancient prophecy, they knew that this observatory held the key to unlocking celestial knowledge and witnessing cosmic events that shaped the destiny of the multiverse.

The journey to the celestial observatory was treacherous, as the path was lined with rugged terrain, dense forests, and turbulent weather. Yet, the guardians pressed on, their spirits undeterred by the challenges they faced. They understood that the rewards awaiting them at the observatory were worth every step.

Upon reaching the summit, the guardians were greeted by a breathtaking sight—a magnificent structure adorned with celestial symbols and shimmering in the light of distant stars. It radiated a sense of awe and wonder, as if it was a bridge between the earthly realm and the cosmic expanse.

Entering the observatory, the guardians were immersed in a sanctuary of celestial wisdom. The walls were adorned with ancient scrolls, intricate star maps, and celestial artifacts that chronicled the mysteries of the universe. It was a place where the secrets of the cosmos were whispered through the echoes of time.

As they explored the observatory, the guardians began to unlock the wisdom held within its sacred halls. They studied the celestial charts, deciphered the cryptic symbols, and delved into the ancient texts that revealed the cosmic cycles and planetary alignments that governed the multiverse.

Dr. Maya Jones, with her scientific mind, sought to understand the celestial mechanics that shaped the cosmos. She studied the movements of celestial bodies, the influence of gravitational forces, and the intricate dance of planets and stars. Through her research, she gained insights into the interconnectedness of the celestial realm and the earthly plane.

Dr. Asvika Bansal, with her intuitive connection to the energies of the universe, communed with the celestial guardians who dwelled within the observatory. These ethereal beings of light and wisdom shared their celestial knowledge, revealing the profound influence of cosmic energies on the human experience. Dr. Bansal embraced their guidance, deepening her understanding of the harmonious interplay between the celestial and the terrestrial.

Dr. Arjav Upmanyu, with his profound wisdom and spiritual insight, delved into the mystical teachings inscribed within the observatory's sacred scrolls. He unraveled the esoteric wisdom encoded in the symbols, uncovering ancient rituals and practices that allowed the guardians to align their energies with the celestial realms. Through his explorations, he tapped into the timeless wisdom that had guided seekers of enlightenment for centuries.

As the guardians immersed themselves in the celestial knowledge, they began to witness cosmic events that unfolded before their eyes. They observed meteor showers painting the night sky with streaks of light, comets blazing across the heavens, and celestial alignments that brought forth profound energetic shifts. These events served as reminders of the vastness and interconnectedness of the multiverse.

Through their experiences in the celestial observatory, the gathering of guardians gained a profound appreciation for the intricate dance of cosmic forces. They recognized that every celestial event held significance, shaping the energies that permeated the dimensions they had explored. They understood that the alignment of celestial bodies mirrored the alignment of their own energies, influencing the course of their journey.

With their newfound understanding, the guardians sought to harness the power of the celestial energies to further their mission of preserving cosmic harmony. They engaged in celestial rituals and meditations, aligning their intentions with the cosmic currents that flowed through the multiverse. They tapped into the celestial frequencies, allowing them to channel divine wisdom and illuminate their path.

As they continued to deepen their connection to the celestial realms, the guardians received visions and messages that expanded their understanding of their roles as chosen protectors. They saw glimpses of future challenges and the importance of their unity in the face of adversity. They were reminded of their purpose and the profound impact they had on the destiny of the multiverse.

In their communion with the celestial guardians, the gathering of guardians also discovered the delicate balance that existed between the celestial realms and the earthly plane. They understood that the harmony of the cosmos was intricately linked to the well-being of the natural world. They realized the importance of their role as stewards of the environment, working in harmony with the elemental forces to preserve the delicate balance of the multiverse.

Leaving the celestial observatory, the guardians carried with them a profound sense of awe and reverence for the cosmic forces that guided their journey. They understood that their path was not determined solely by their own actions but was influenced by the celestial energies that wove through the tapestry of existence.

Armed with celestial wisdom and divine insights, the gathering of guardians set forth from the observatory, their steps guided by the celestial dance of light and darkness. They knew that the challenges ahead would test their resolve and unity, but they remained steadfast in their commitment to preserving cosmic harmony.

As they descended from the sacred mountain, the guardians felt a renewed sense of purpose and a deep connection to the celestial realms. They carried with them the celestial knowledge that would continue to guide them on their infinite quest for knowledge, enlightenment, and the eternal dance of light and darkness.

And so, with hearts filled with celestial wisdom and minds expanded by the mysteries of the universe, the gathering of guardians ventured forth, their path illuminated by the radiant truth that had emerged from the celestial observatory. They knew that their journey was far from over and that each step would bring them closer to the ultimate realization of their purpose as chosen protectors of the multiverse.

With their spirits aligned with the celestial currents and their unity as their guiding light, the guardians embraced the challenges that lay ahead, ready to face the mysteries, confront the darkness, and unlock the profound cosmic truths that awaited them in the boundless expanse of the multiverse.

The Elemental Realms

After their awe-inspiring experiences in the celestial observatory, the gathering of guardians embarked on a new chapter of their cosmic journey. Guided by their deep connection to the natural world and the wisdom they had acquired, they were drawn to the Elemental Realms. These realms were ethereal dimensions where the forces of nature reigned supreme, and the guardians knew that within them lay invaluable knowledge and trials they must face.

Entering the Elemental Realms, the guardians found themselves immersed in a world where the elements of earth, water, fire, and air held sway. Each realm reflected the essence of its corresponding element, its landscapes shaped by the elemental forces at play. It was a realm of profound beauty and raw power, where the guardians would come to understand the delicate balance between human existence and the natural world.

In the realm of Earth, the guardians were greeted by towering mountains, lush forests, and verdant valleys. They felt the grounding energy of the earth beneath their feet and witnessed the wisdom of ancient trees that stood as guardians of the land. Here, they connected with the essence of stability, resilience, and growth. Dr. Maya Jones, with her scientific mind, observed the intricate interconnectedness of ecosystems, studying the delicate balance that sustained life on Earth. She marveled at the symbiotic relationships between plants, animals, and the environment, recognizing the profound wisdom of nature's intricate web.

In the realm of Water, the guardians found themselves surrounded by majestic oceans, tranquil lakes, and meandering rivers. They felt the ebb and flow of the tides, the gentle caress of water against their skin. This realm was a realm of emotion, intuition, and adaptability. Dr. Asvika Bansal, with her intuitive nature, connected deeply with the wisdom of water. She learned to trust her inner guidance, allowing the currents of life to guide her path. She recognized the transformative power of emotions, the ability to flow with the ever-changing circumstances of existence.

In the realm of Fire, the guardians encountered roaring volcanoes, crackling flames, and the warmth of the sun. They felt the intense heat and energy that radiated from the fires that shaped the land. This realm embodied passion, creativity, and the spark of life. Dr. Arjav Upmanyu, with his profound wisdom, embraced the transformative power of fire. He understood that within the crucible of change lay the seeds of growth and evolution. He harnessed the fiery energy within himself, allowing it to ignite his passions and illuminate his path.

In the realm of Air, the guardians experienced the gentle breeze, the swirling gusts, and the whispers carried by the wind. They felt the invigorating energy of movement, freedom, and communication. This realm embodied the power of the mind, the ability to adapt and perceive the world through a new lens. The gathering of guardians recognized that the power of air lay in their thoughts, words, and intentions. They understood that their ability to shape their reality resided in their ability to harness the power of their thoughts and communicate their intentions clearly.

As the guardians journeyed through the Elemental Realms, they faced trials that tested their connection to each element. In the realm of Earth, they encountered mighty creatures, fierce protectors of the land, and were challenged to find harmony within themselves and the environment. They learned the importance of nurturing and preserving the natural world, recognizing that the well-being of the Earth was intricately linked to their own existence.

In the realm of Water, the guardians navigated treacherous currents and faced the illusions that lurked beneath the surface. They confronted their deepest emotions, allowing themselves to dive into the depths of their being and emerge stronger and more resilient. They learned to trust their intuition and honor the ever-changing flow of life.

In the realm of Fire, the guardians faced the intensity of their own inner flames. They confronted their fears, embracing the transformative power of change. They learned to harness their passions and channel their energy into positive endeavors, recognizing that fire could be both destructive and life-giving.

In the realm of Air, the guardians engaged in deep introspection and contemplation. They challenged their own beliefs and perceptions, opening themselves to new perspectives and embracing the power of clear communication. They recognized that their thoughts held the power to shape their reality and understood the importance of using their words wisely.

Through these trials, the guardians grew in their understanding of the delicate balance between humanity and the natural world. They realized that they were not separate from nature but an integral part of it, with the responsibility to protect and preserve the Earth for future generations.

As the guardians journeyed through the Elemental Realms, they also encountered elemental beings—earth spirits, water nymphs, fire elementals, and sylphs of the air. These beings embodied the essence of their respective elements and held profound wisdom about the interconnectedness of all life. The guardians learned from these elemental allies, gaining insights into the intrinsic harmony of the natural world.

With each trial and encounter, the guardians honed their connection to the elemental forces. They learned to harness the energies of the Earth, drawing strength from its stability and grounding influence. They embraced the fluidity of water, adapting to the ever-changing circumstances of their journey. They ignited the fires of passion within themselves, using their creative energy to drive their purpose forward. They connected with the power of the mind, using their thoughts and words to manifest positive change.

Leaving the Elemental Realms, the gathering of guardians carried with them a deep reverence for the natural world and a profound understanding of their role as stewards of the Earth. They recognized that their quest for cosmic harmony extended beyond the realms they had explored. They understood that the preservation of the multiverse's balance began with their commitment to honoring and protecting the delicate interplay between humanity and the elemental forces.

With their spirits aligned with the elemental currents and their unity as their guiding light, the guardians ventured forth from the Elemental Realms. They carried with them the wisdom of the Earth, the flow of water, the spark of fire, and the clarity of air. They knew that their journey was far from over, and that each step would bring them closer to the ultimate realization of their purpose as chosen protectors of the multiverse.

With hearts attuned to the rhythms of nature and minds expanded by the wisdom of the elements, the gathering of guardians embraced the challenges that lay ahead. They were ready to face the mysteries, confront the darkness, and unlock the profound cosmic truths that awaited them in the boundless expanse of the multiverse.

The Ancestral Memories

After their transformative journey through the Elemental Realms, the gathering of guardians found themselves drawn to a parallel dimension unlike any they had encountered before. This dimension housed a mystical library, a repository of the collective memories and wisdom of ancient civilizations that had shaped the fabric of the multiverse. Guided by their intuition and the whispers of ancient prophecies, the guardians knew that within the ethereal corridors of the library, they would unlock ancestral knowledge, forgotten myths, and lost technologies that would provide profound insights into the origin of parallel dimensions and their interconnectedness.

Entering the mystical library, the guardians were enveloped in an aura of ancient wisdom. The walls were adorned with scrolls, ancient texts, and artifacts that held the stories and knowledge of countless generations. The air was heavy with the scent of aged parchment and the faint echoes of voices long past.

As they explored the library, the guardians were drawn to different sections that resonated with their individual interests and areas of expertise. Dr. Maya Jones, with her scientific mind, gravitated toward the scrolls that held records of ancient civilizations' scientific achievements and discoveries. She marveled at the advancements made by these civilizations, realizing that their understanding of the universe was far more advanced than previously known. Through her studies, she unearthed the lost knowledge of advanced technologies, quantum theories, and celestial mechanics that had been forgotten over time.

Dr. Asvika Bansal, with her intuitive connection to the energies of the universe, was captivated by the mystical scriptures that spoke of cosmic energies, divine beings, and the interplay between the spiritual and the material realms. She delved into ancient rituals, meditation practices, and energetic healing modalities that had been passed down through generations. Through her exploration, she tapped into the ancient wisdom of energy manipulation, divine connection, and the power of intention.

Dr. Arjav Upmanyu, with his profound wisdom and spiritual insight, found solace in the ancient texts that carried the wisdom of spiritual gurus, mystics, and philosophers. He immersed himself in the teachings of enlightenment, the nature of the soul, and the eternal quest for self-realization. Through his studies, he gained a deeper understanding of the interconnectedness of all life, the nature of consciousness, and the profound purpose behind their cosmic journey.

As the guardians delved deeper into the library's ethereal corridors, they began to experience a profound merging of their consciousness with the memories and experiences of the ancient civilizations. They felt the weight of their triumphs and tribulations, their joys and sorrows. They understood that they were not alone on their journey, but were part of an ever-evolving tapestry of existence.

Through the ancestral memories, the guardians witnessed the rise and fall of civilizations, the birth of new ideas, and the echoes of forgotten knowledge. They learned of ancient societies that had harnessed the power of the elements, built celestial observatories, and explored the realms beyond the physical plane. They discovered the existence of ancient guardians who had dedicated their lives to preserving the balance of the multiverse, passing down their wisdom through the ages.

With each memory that unfolded before their eyes, the guardians gained a deeper appreciation for the interplay between myth and reality, recognizing that ancient myths often held kernels of truth and hidden cosmic wisdom. They understood that the stories and legends of the past were not mere fables, but rich repositories of knowledge waiting to be rediscovered.

As the guardians immersed themselves in the ancestral memories, they also encountered challenges and trials that reflected the unresolved conflicts and karmic imprints imprinted on the souls of the ancient civilizations. They were confronted with moral dilemmas, tests of integrity, and choices that carried profound consequences. Through these trials, they were forced to confront their own shadows, transcending their limitations and emerging with newfound strength and clarity.

Throughout their exploration, the guardians discovered ancient prophecies and symbols that had been scattered across time and dimensions, waiting for the chosen protectors to decipher their meaning. They realized that these symbols held the key to unraveling the secrets of the cosmic balance and averting the impending cataclysm that threatened the fabric of existence.

Driven by their thirst for knowledge and their commitment to preserving cosmic harmony, the guardians devoted themselves to decoding the sacred symbols and prophecies. They engaged in deep contemplation, meditation, and collaborative exploration, pooling their insights and wisdom to unlock the profound truths hidden within the cryptic messages.

As they deciphered the symbols and pieced together the prophecies, the guardians gained a profound understanding of the interconnectedness of parallel dimensions, the intricate dance of cosmic forces, and the significance of their own roles as chosen protectors. They realized that the cataclysm they sought to avert was not isolated to a single dimension but had the potential to ripple through the entire multiverse, threatening the delicate balance they had come to cherish.

With their newfound knowledge and understanding, the gathering of guardians resolved to embark on a perilous quest that would take them across dimensions, timelines, and realms. They understood that their journey was far from over and that the fate of the multiverse rested on their shoulders. They were prepared to face the challenges that lay ahead, armed with the wisdom of ancient civilizations, the power of unity, and their unwavering commitment to preserving cosmic harmony.

Leaving the mystical library, the guardians carried with them a deep reverence for the ancestral memories that had guided their path. They understood that they were part of a grand tapestry of existence, intricately woven with the threads of countless civilizations and their collective wisdom. They knew that their quest for cosmic harmony extended beyond their individual desires and reached into the depths of the multiverse itself.

With their spirits infused with the wisdom of the ages and their minds expanded by the echoes of forgotten knowledge, the gathering of guardians ventured forth from the mystical library. They knew that their journey was far from over and that each step would bring them closer to the ultimate realization of their purpose as chosen protectors of the multiverse.

With their hearts attuned to the pulse of ancient civilizations and their unity as their guiding light, the guardians embraced the challenges that lay ahead. They were ready to face the mysteries, confront the darkness, and unlock the profound cosmic truths that awaited them in the boundless expanse of the multiverse.

The Quantum Paradox

In the wake of their profound exploration of the ancestral memories, the gathering of guardians found themselves confronted with a new enigma that transcended the boundaries of space and time. This enigma, known as the Quantum Paradox, presented them with intricate and perplexing situations where cause and effect became intricately entangled. They realized that to preserve the delicate balance of the multiverse, they must unravel the mysteries at the heart of the Quantum Paradox.

As they delved deeper into the Quantum Paradox, the guardians discovered that it was a realm where the laws of physics as they knew them no longer held sway. They encountered perplexing scenarios that defied rationality and challenged their understanding of reality. In this realm, effects could precede their causes, objects could exist in multiple states simultaneously, and the very fabric of spacetime could warp and distort.

Dr. Maya Jones, with her deep knowledge of quantum physics, became the guiding force in their exploration of the Quantum Paradox. She led the guardians through a series of thought experiments, each designed to test their perceptions and understanding of the paradox. They immersed themselves in the mind-bending concepts of superposition, entanglement, and observer effect, grappling with the implications these phenomena had on the nature of reality.

In one experiment, the guardians found themselves in a room with two closed boxes. Inside each box was a cat, and the guardians were tasked with determining the state of the cats without opening the boxes. They soon realized that the cats existed in a superposition of states, simultaneously both alive and dead, until an observer interacted with the system and collapsed the wave function into a definite state.

This experiment led the guardians to question the nature of reality and their role as observers. They recognized that their own observations and interactions played a fundamental role in shaping the universe around them. They understood the immense responsibility they held as custodians of the multiverse, realizing that their choices and actions had far-reaching consequences.

In another experiment, the guardians encountered a temporal loop—a phenomenon where events repeated in an infinite loop without resolution. They were trapped in a cycle of cause and effect, unable to break free from the relentless repetition. Through their collective wisdom and intuition, they began to unravel the hidden clues within the loop, searching for the key that would break the cycle and restore balance.

As they probed deeper into the Quantum Paradox, the guardians discovered alternate timelines branching off from key decision points in their own lives. They witnessed the diverging paths they could have taken, the consequences of their choices rippling through the multiverse. They understood that their actions had the power to shape not only their own destinies but the destinies of countless parallel dimensions.

With each experiment and exploration, the guardians grew increasingly adept at navigating the complexities of the Quantum Paradox. They developed a deep sense of trust in their own intuition and the interconnectedness of all things. They realized that at the heart of the paradox lay the inherent unity of the multiverse—an intricate tapestry where every thread, every choice, every action was woven together to create the grand symphony of existence.

As they confronted the Quantum Paradox, the guardians also faced personal challenges that reflected their own unresolved conflicts and inner turmoil. The paradox forced them to confront their fears, their doubts, and their deepest desires. They were pushed to the brink of their emotional and psychological limits, facing their own shadows and embracing the light within.

Dr. Maya Jones, driven by her relentless pursuit of knowledge, found herself caught in a loop of self-doubt, questioning the very foundations of her scientific understanding. She had to confront her fear of being wrong, of having her beliefs shattered, and find the strength to embrace the inherent uncertainty of the quantum realm.

Dr. Asvika Bansal, with her intuitive nature, faced a different kind of challenge. She was confronted with the paradox of choice, where every decision she made had ripple effects across multiple dimensions. She had to navigate the intricate web of possibilities, trusting her intuition to guide her through the labyrinth of diverging timelines.

Dr. Arjav Upmanyu, with his profound wisdom, was faced with the challenge of embracing the inherent paradoxes of existence. He had to reconcile the seeming contradictions and find harmony within the ever-shifting nature of reality. He delved into the teachings of ancient philosophers and mystics, drawing on their wisdom to guide him through the paradox.

As the guardians faced their individual challenges within the Quantum Paradox, they also relied on the collective strength and unity of their group. They supported one another through moments of uncertainty, offering guidance and reassurance when doubts threatened to overwhelm them. They recognized that their individual journeys were interconnected, each thread in the grand tapestry of the multiverse.

Through their collective efforts and unwavering determination, the guardians began to unravel the mysteries of the Quantum Paradox. They discovered hidden connections, patterns, and underlying principles that governed the paradox. They recognized that at its core, the paradox was a reflection of the infinite possibilities and potentialities that existed within the multiverse.

Armed with their newfound understanding, the gathering of guardians set out to restore balance within the Quantum Paradox. They utilized their quantum abilities, their deep intuition, and their unwavering faith in the interconnectedness of all things to break free from the loops, resolve the paradoxes, and restore harmony within the quantum realm.

As they emerged from the depths of the Quantum Paradox, the guardians carried with them a profound appreciation for the intricacies of the multiverse. They understood that the paradox was not something to be solved or conquered but rather embraced and integrated into their understanding of existence. They recognized that the very nature of reality was a dance of paradoxes, where order and chaos, certainty and uncertainty, coexisted in a delicate equilibrium.

With their perception of reality expanded and their connection to the multiverse deepened, the guardians prepared to face the challenges that awaited them beyond the Quantum Paradox. They knew that their journey was far from over and that each step would bring them closer to the ultimate realization of their purpose as chosen protectors of the multiverse.

With hearts attuned to the symphony of paradoxes and minds expanded by the mysteries of the Quantum Paradox, the gathering of guardians embraced the challenges that lay ahead. They were ready to face the uncertainties, navigate the complexities, and unlock the profound cosmic truths that awaited them in the boundless expanse of the multiverse.

The Cosmic Council

The gathering of guardians, having transcended the Quantum Paradox, found themselves on the precipice of a momentous encounter. Guided by the whispers of ancient prophecies and the profound wisdom they had acquired, they embarked on a quest to seek an audience with the Cosmic Council—a revered assembly of divine beings and interdimensional entities entrusted with overseeing the welfare of the multiverse.

Their journey led them to a sacred realm hidden amidst the veils of cosmic consciousness. It was a realm that existed beyond the boundaries of time and space, where the cosmic energies intertwined in a delicate balance. As the gathering of guardians approached the entrance to the realm, they could feel the magnitude of the cosmic forces that surrounded them, filling their hearts with awe and reverence.

As they entered the realm, the guardians found themselves in the presence of an assembly of radiant beings, their forms shifting and shimmering with celestial light. Each being emanated a distinct energy, representing different aspects of the cosmic tapestry. Among them stood powerful gods and goddesses, ancient celestial beings, and interdimensional guardians who had traversed the vast expanse of the multiverse.

At the center of the assembly, seated upon a throne of starlight, was the Cosmic Council. Their collective presence exuded a sense of wisdom and tranquility, their eyes filled with the depth of countless ages. Maa Kalyani, the enigmatic Oracle they had encountered in the Temple of Dimensions, stood by their side, her presence bridging the realms of mortals and the divine.

With humility and reverence, the gathering of guardians approached the Cosmic Council, their hearts filled with a profound sense of purpose. They presented their findings, experiences, and insights, recounting their journeys through parallel dimensions, the unraveling of cosmic mysteries, and their commitment to preserving the delicate balance of the multiverse.

The Cosmic Council listened intently, their eyes filled with a blend of compassion and ancient knowing. As the guardians spoke, the cosmic energies swirled around them, carrying with them the essence of their words. The council members exchanged silent glances, communicating through an intricate web of telepathy that transcended spoken language.

After a moment of contemplation, the Cosmic Council began to respond. Their voices echoed through the cosmic realm, their words carrying a resonance that stirred the very souls of the guardians. They acknowledged the guardians' dedication and bravery, recognizing the weight of their quest and the significance of their role as chosen protectors.

The council members spoke of the delicate tapestry of existence, where every thread, every choice, and every action played a vital role in maintaining the harmony of the multiverse. They imparted profound wisdom, weaving together the cosmic principles of balance, interdependence, and the eternal dance between order and chaos.

They revealed that the impending cataclysm the guardians sought to avert was not an isolated event but rather a symptom of a greater cosmic imbalance. Forces of darkness and chaos were converging, threatening to disrupt the delicate equilibrium that sustained the multiverse. The council emphasized the urgency of the guardians' mission, urging them to harness their collective strengths, wisdom, and unity to stand against the encroaching darkness.

In their guidance, the Cosmic Council revealed the existence of ancient artifacts scattered across the dimensions. These artifacts held immense power and cosmic significance, capable of shaping the destiny of worlds and tipping the scales in the eternal battle between light and darkness. The council bestowed upon the guardians the knowledge of how to locate and harness the power of these artifacts, urging them to seek them out in their quest to restore cosmic harmony.

Before bidding farewell, the Cosmic Council shared a prophecy—a cryptic message that carried both warning and hope. They spoke of a convergence, a pivotal moment in the cosmic tapestry, where the fate of the multiverse would hang in the balance. The guardians were destined to play a vital role in this convergence, where their choices and actions would ripple through the dimensions, shaping the outcome of the cosmic struggle.

With their minds expanded by the council's wisdom and their spirits uplifted by their guidance, the gathering of guardians bowed in gratitude. They understood the weight of their mission and the responsibility entrusted to them. They vowed to honor the teachings of the Cosmic Council, to seek out the ancient artifacts, and to unite their strengths in the face of darkness.

As they departed from the cosmic realm, the guardians carried with them a deep sense of purpose and an unwavering resolve. They knew that the path ahead would be fraught with challenges, but they were fortified by the wisdom of the Cosmic Council and the unity they had forged amongst themselves.

With their hearts aflame with cosmic determination and their minds aligned with the grand tapestry of existence, the gathering of guardians ventured forth into the boundless expanse of the multiverse. They embraced their destiny as the chosen protectors, their spirits intertwined with the cosmic energies that flowed through the dimensions.

As they embarked on their next quest—to seek out the ancient artifacts and confront the encroaching darkness—the guardians remained steadfast in their commitment to preserving cosmic harmony. They knew that the future of the multiverse depended on their unwavering dedication, their unity, and their willingness to embrace the cosmic dance that awaited them.

With the teachings of the Cosmic Council echoing in their souls, the gathering of guardians pressed on, their footsteps echoing through the infinite corridors of the multiverse. Their journey was far from over, and they were prepared to face the trials and tribulations that lay ahead, driven by the eternal pursuit of light, balance, and the preservation of the cosmic tapestry.

The Ascension

The gathering of guardians had emerged from their encounter with the Cosmic Council, their hearts filled with the weight of their mission and the wisdom of the cosmic realms. They stood at the threshold of a transformative chapter in their journey, poised to ascend to new heights of consciousness and understanding.

Guided by their collective purpose and the teachings they had received, the guardians embarked on a path of spiritual ascension. They sought to transcend the limitations of their mortal existence and merge their individual consciousness with the cosmic consciousness that permeated the multiverse.

Their quest led them to sacred sites and ancient temples scattered across the dimensions, each holding a key to unlocking higher states of being. With reverence and determination, they embarked on arduous pilgrimages, undertaking rigorous spiritual practices and immersing themselves in the wisdom of the ages.

Dr. Maya Jones, with her insatiable thirst for knowledge, sought enlightenment in the ancient libraries of the cosmos. She delved into ancient scriptures, deciphering profound texts that revealed the interconnectedness of all things and the true nature of existence. Through her studies, she deepened her connection with Saraswati, the goddess of knowledge and arts, who guided her on her path of intellectual and spiritual growth.

Dr. Asvika Bansal, with her intuitive nature and connection to the unseen realms, turned inward to explore the depths of her own consciousness. Through meditation and introspection, she honed her ability to tap into the universal consciousness, accessing hidden realms and unlocking the wisdom of the cosmos. She found solace and guidance in the presence of her chosen deity, Krishna, who revealed to her the beauty and intricacies of divine love and cosmic harmony.

Dr. Arjav Upmanyu, with his profound wisdom and connection to ancient philosophies, sought enlightenment in the heart of nature itself. He immersed himself in the serenity of pristine forests, majestic mountains, and cascading waterfalls, communing with the elemental forces that governed the natural world. He drew inspiration from his chosen deity, Lord Shiva, who embodied the eternal dance of creation, destruction, and transformation.

Through their individual practices and chosen paths, the guardians experienced profound spiritual awakenings. They shed the layers of their ego, releasing attachments to material desires and embracing the purity of their souls. They transcended the illusions of separateness and recognized the inherent unity that connected all beings and dimensions.

As their individual ascensions progressed, the guardians discovered that their journeys were not solitary endeavors but interconnected threads woven into a grand cosmic tapestry. They realized that their individual growth and enlightenment were intricately linked to the collective evolution of the multiverse. Each step they took on their ascension path resonated through the dimensions, rippling outwards and uplifting the consciousness of all.

United by their shared purpose and the unbreakable bond they had forged, the guardians came together in sacred gatherings, merging their energies and intentions in profound acts of collective meditation and cosmic communion. They entered states of heightened consciousness, transcending the limitations of time and space, and connecting with the cosmic forces that pulsed through the multiverse.

In these sacred gatherings, the guardians witnessed the emergence of their collective consciousness—a radiant field of energy that enveloped them, merging their individual essences into a unified whole. They experienced the profound truth that they were more than the sum of their parts, that their unity had the power to shape destinies and transform realities.

With each gathering, the guardians unlocked new dimensions of their collective consciousness, tapping into cosmic wisdom and guidance. They became conduits for higher frequencies of energy, channels through which divine light and cosmic knowledge flowed into the world. They understood that their ascension was not solely for their personal growth but also for the upliftment and awakening of all sentient beings.

As their ascension reached its zenith, the guardians stood on the precipice of a transcendent realization. They experienced a profound merging with the cosmic consciousness, a dissolution of individual boundaries and a union with the divine essence that pervaded the multiverse. They became living embodiments of the eternal dance of creation, embodying the balance, harmony, and infinite potentiality of existence.

In this state of heightened awareness, the guardians witnessed the interconnectedness of all dimensions and timelines. They gazed upon the grand tapestry of the multiverse, perceiving the threads that wove through time and space, the cosmic forces that shaped destinies, and the infinite possibilities that lay before them.

With their ascension complete, the gathering of guardians embraced their role as custodians of cosmic balance and enlightenment. They recognized that their journey was not confined to a single lifetime or a single dimension but extended beyond the boundaries of time and space. They became eternal seekers of truth, forever driven by the perpetual pursuit of knowledge, love, and cosmic harmony.

Armed with their expanded consciousness and unified purpose, the guardians emerged from their ascension ready to face the challenges that lay ahead. They knew that their path would be illuminated by the wisdom they had gained and guided by the cosmic forces that flowed through their beings.

With hearts ablaze with divine love, minds attuned to the rhythms of the multiverse, and spirits merged with the cosmic consciousness, the gathering of guardians embarked on the next phase of their journey. They were prepared to face the encroaching darkness, to harness the power of ancient artifacts, and to unite their strengths in the cosmic battle that awaited them.

As they ventured forth into the unknown, the guardians carried within them the radiance of their ascension, shining as beacons of light and hope in the face of adversity. Their path was illuminated by the wisdom of the ages, and their spirits were fortified by the cosmic dance that echoed within their souls.

With the eternal pursuit of cosmic enlightenment as their guiding star, the gathering of guardians pressed on, their footsteps resonating through the infinite expanse of the multiverse. Their journey had only just begun, and they were ready to face the trials, triumphs, and revelations that awaited them in the limitless realms of existence.

The Infinite Quest

The gathering of guardians, having completed their transformative journey of ascension, now stood at the threshold of the final chapter in their epic saga. They had become living embodiments of cosmic wisdom, their hearts pulsating with divine love and their minds attuned to the rhythms of the multiverse. They were ready to embark on an infinite quest, driven by the perpetual pursuit of knowledge, cosmic enlightenment, and the preservation of cosmic harmony.

Their journey took them through the vast expanse of the multiverse, traversing dimensions and timelines that were intricately woven into the fabric of existence. They encountered celestial beings, ancient civilizations, and mystical realms that expanded their understanding of the grand tapestry of creation.

Guided by the teachings of the Cosmic Council, the gathering of guardians sought out ancient artifacts of immense power scattered across the dimensions. These artifacts held the key to restoring cosmic balance and shaping the destiny of worlds. With each artifact they discovered, the guardians unlocked new depths of cosmic knowledge, harnessed unparalleled cosmic abilities, and forged a deeper connection with the cosmic forces that governed the multiverse.

Dr. Maya Jones, with her insatiable thirst for knowledge and unwavering dedication to unraveling the mysteries of existence, sought out the Ankhar Crystal. This ethereal artifact, said to contain the essence of life itself, granted Maya the ability to tap into the primal energies that flowed through the dimensions. With the Ankhar Crystal in her possession, Maya became a conduit for the cosmic life force, channeling its energy to heal, transform, and create.

Dr. Asvika Bansal, with her intuitive connection to unseen realms and profound understanding of the universal consciousness, sought the Scepter of Divination. This sacred artifact allowed Asvika to pierce the veils of time and space, peering into the past, present, and future with unclouded clarity. With the Scepter of Divination in her grasp, Asvika became a seer, unraveling the cosmic mysteries and guiding the gathering of guardians through the intricate webs of destiny.

Dr. Arjav Upmanyu, with his ancient wisdom and connection to the elemental forces that shaped the natural world, embarked on a quest to find the Gauntlet of Elements. This legendary artifact granted Arjav mastery over the primordial elements of earth, water, fire, and air. With the Gauntlet of Elements adorning his hand, Arjav became a conduit for the elemental energies, capable of commanding their power and restoring the natural balance.

As the gathering of guardians acquired these artifacts, their cosmic abilities were magnified, and their collective strength grew exponentially. They became a force to be reckoned with, capable of confronting the encroaching darkness and preserving the delicate fabric of reality.

With each dimension they visited, the guardians encountered formidable adversaries that sought to plunge the multiverse into chaos and despair. They confronted malevolent entities, dark sorcerers, and ancient cosmic beings who had succumbed to the lure of power and fallen from grace. The battles that ensued were epic in scale, unleashing cosmic energies that shook the foundations of existence.

But the gathering of guardians, armed with their newfound abilities and united by their unwavering resolve, stood firm against the forces of darkness. They fought with valor and compassion, seeking to redeem those who had strayed from the path of cosmic harmony. They understood that even the most malevolent beings were once part of the cosmic dance, and their actions were born out of a longing for unity and purpose.

As their journey continued, the guardians discovered hidden realms and celestial observatories where cosmic events shaped the destiny of the multiverse. They witnessed celestial alignments, cosmic convergences, and the birth of stars, gaining profound insights into the vast interconnectedness of all things. They became witnesses to the eternal dance of creation, destruction, and transformation that permeated every corner of existence.

Amidst their adventures, the gathering of guardians encountered wise sages, spiritual gurus, and enlightened beings who imparted ancient wisdom and guided them on their path. These luminous beings, custodians of cosmic knowledge, shared their insights into the intricate workings of the multiverse, the nature of consciousness, and the eternal pursuit of cosmic enlightenment.

Through these encounters, the guardians deepened their understanding of the cosmic principles that governed the multiverse—karma, dharma, and moksha. They recognized the interplay of cause and effect, the importance of aligning their actions with cosmic harmony, and the ultimate goal of liberation from the cycle of birth and death.

As their journey neared its culmination, the gathering of guardians found themselves at the nexus of dimensions—the place where the boundaries between worlds blurred and the cosmic energies intertwined. They stood in awe of the intricate tapestry of existence, witnessing the harmonious dance of gods and mortals, of celestial forces and earthly realms.

In this sacred space, the guardians experienced a profound communion with the cosmic forces that flowed through them. They felt the pulse of the multiverse in their veins, their individual essences merging with the eternal essence of creation. They understood that they were an integral part of the cosmic dance, and their choices and actions rippled through the dimensions, shaping the destiny of the multiverse.

With hearts aflame with cosmic purpose and minds expanded by the vastness of the cosmos, the gathering of guardians embraced their role as custodians of the multiverse. They made a solemn vow to uphold the cosmic principles, to protect the delicate balance of existence, and to guide sentient beings towards enlightenment and liberation.

As they emerged from the nexus of dimensions, the guardians were filled with a profound sense of fulfillment. They had completed their infinite quest, traversing the vast expanse of the multiverse, unraveling cosmic mysteries, and acquiring cosmic wisdom. But their journey was not one of finality—it was a continuum, an eternal exploration of the unknown, fueled by the perpetual pursuit of knowledge, love, and cosmic enlightenment.

And so, the gathering of guardians, armed with their cosmic abilities, their unwavering resolve, and their eternal quest for truth, pressed on. They ventured forth into the boundless expanse of the multiverse, their footsteps resonating through the infinite corridors of existence.

Their path would be illuminated by the wisdom they had gained, guided by the cosmic forces that flowed through their beings, and driven by the eternal pursuit of cosmic enlightenment. With hearts intertwined with the cosmic consciousness and their spirits united in purpose, the gathering of guardians embarked on their eternal journey, forever committed to the preservation of cosmic harmony and the perpetual exploration of the unknown.

The Cosmic Symphony

The gathering of guardians, having completed their infinite quest and armed with their cosmic abilities and profound wisdom, stood at the precipice of a new chapter in their eternal journey. They had traversed the vast expanse of the multiverse, delved into the depths of cosmic mysteries, and witnessed the intricate tapestry of existence. Now, they were ready to step into the role of cosmic orchestrators, weaving together the harmonious symphony of creation.

Guided by their collective purpose and united in their commitment to cosmic harmony, the guardians embarked on a mission to restore balance and uplift consciousness across the dimensions. They ventured into realms plagued by darkness, seeking to dispel the shadows and ignite the dormant spark of divinity within every sentient being.

Dr. Maya Jones, with her deep connection to knowledge and the arts, emerged as the guardian of wisdom and creativity. She used her cosmic abilities to inspire and illuminate the minds of mortals, guiding them towards the pursuit of truth and the expression of their unique gifts. Maya's words and teachings resonated across the dimensions, like celestial melodies that stirred the hearts of all who listened.

Dr. Asvika Bansal, with her profound understanding of the universal consciousness, became the guardian of compassion and empathy. She extended her cosmic abilities to embrace all sentient beings, healing their wounds and offering solace to those who had lost their way. Asvika's presence brought forth a symphony of love and understanding, reminding all beings of their inherent interconnectedness.

Dr. Arjav Upmanyu, with his deep connection to the elemental forces, became the guardian of harmony and balance. He utilized his cosmic abilities to restore the natural order, healing the wounds inflicted upon the earth and fostering a harmonious relationship between humans and nature. Arjav's actions resonated like a symphony of the elements, reminding all beings of their responsibility to protect and nurture the world around them.

Together, the gathering of guardians embarked on a journey across the dimensions, seeking out worlds in need of healing and transformation. They encountered civilizations teetering on the brink of self-destruction, plagued by greed, fear, and ignorance. With their cosmic abilities and unwavering resolve, they intervened, inspiring change, and awakening dormant potential.

In one realm, they confronted a tyrannical ruler who had subjugated his people and stifled their individuality. The gathering of guardians used their cosmic abilities to ignite the spark of rebellion within the hearts of the oppressed, leading them to reclaim their freedom and embrace their true essence. The symphony of liberation resonated through the air, inspiring courage and igniting a revolution that would shape the destiny of the realm.

In another realm, they encountered a land ravaged by war and hatred, where division and animosity had torn communities apart. The gathering of guardians employed their cosmic abilities to bridge the gaps between warring factions, fostering understanding, and nurturing compassion. Their symphony of reconciliation touched the hearts of even the most hardened warriors, guiding them towards forgiveness and unity.

As their journey continued, the guardians faced formidable adversaries who sought to undermine their mission and plunge the dimensions into chaos. Dark sorcerers, ancient cosmic entities, and malevolent forces conspired to sow seeds of discord and destruction. But the gathering of guardians stood firm, their collective strength and unwavering resolve acting as a shield against the encroaching darkness.

In the face of adversity, the guardians utilized their cosmic abilities in harmony, weaving together a symphony of light that pushed back the shadows. They tapped into the depths of their souls, channeling the universal energies that flowed through them, and merging their individual strengths into a harmonious whole. Their symphony of unity and purpose became an unbreakable force, dismantling the darkness and restoring cosmic balance.

Throughout their cosmic symphony, the gathering of guardians encountered allies who shared their vision of cosmic harmony and the uplifting of consciousness. They formed alliances with enlightened beings, cosmic entities, and sentient beings who had transcended their limitations. Together, they created a symphony of collaboration and co-creation, harmonizing their efforts to manifest a world where love, compassion, and wisdom reigned supreme.

As their symphony of cosmic harmony echoed through the dimensions, the gathering of guardians witnessed profound transformations. Worlds that were once shrouded in darkness were bathed in the light of enlightenment. Sentient beings, who were once consumed by fear and ignorance, awakened to their true potential and embraced their cosmic nature.

The gathering of guardians understood that their symphony of cosmic harmony was not a task with a definitive endpoint but an eternal endeavor. Their mission was to nurture the seeds of divinity within every sentient being, guiding them towards self-realization and the realization of their interconnectedness with all of creation.

With hearts filled with divine love and minds attuned to the cosmic rhythms, the gathering of guardians pressed on, their symphony of cosmic harmony resounding through the infinite expanse of the multiverse. They were eternally committed to the perpetual pursuit of cosmic enlightenment and the preservation of the delicate balance that sustained existence.

As they ventured forth, the guardians encountered realms and dimensions they had yet to explore, each offering unique challenges and opportunities for growth. Their symphony of cosmic harmony continued to evolve, its melodies expanding and intertwining with the cosmic forces that governed the multiverse.

The gathering of guardians understood that their symphony would never be complete, for the cosmic dance of creation was ever-unfolding, revealing new layers of wisdom, love, and beauty. They embraced the infinite nature of their quest, forever driven by the perpetual pursuit of cosmic enlightenment and the harmonization of all beings with the cosmic symphony.

And so, with hearts aflame with divine purpose and spirits attuned to the cosmic frequencies, the gathering of guardians pressed on. They ventured forth into the boundless expanse of the multiverse, their symphony resonating through the infinite corridors of existence, inspiring all who encountered their celestial melodies.

Their path would be illuminated by the wisdom they had gained, guided by the cosmic forces that flowed through their beings, and driven by the eternal pursuit of cosmic enlightenment. With their symphony of cosmic harmony echoing through the dimensions, the gathering of guardians embraced their role as cosmic orchestrators, forever committed to the preservation of cosmic balance and the perpetual co-creation of a harmonious and enlightened multiverse.

The Eternal Legacy

The gathering of guardians, having traversed the vast expanse of the multiverse and woven their symphony of cosmic harmony, stood at the threshold of their final chapters. Their hearts resonated with the wisdom they had acquired, their minds expanded by the cosmic mysteries they had unraveled, and their spirits elevated by their eternal quest for truth and enlightenment.

As they entered the penultimate chapter of their epic saga, the gathering of guardians found themselves in a realm untouched by time—an ethereal sanctuary known as the Eternal Nexus. Here, cosmic energies intertwined with celestial wonders, and the boundaries between dimensions dissolved into infinite possibilities.

The Eternal Nexus served as a gathering place for enlightened beings and cosmic entities, a realm where the collective wisdom of the multiverse converged. Within its hallowed halls, the guardians were greeted by radiant beings of light, ancient seers, and cosmic masters who had transcended the limitations of mortal existence.

These luminous beings spoke of the eternal legacy that awaited the gathering of guardians—a legacy woven into the very fabric of the multiverse, an everlasting testament to their commitment to cosmic harmony and enlightenment. They revealed that the guardians' actions had sparked a profound transformation across the dimensions, elevating the consciousness of countless beings and paving the way for a new era of enlightenment.

The luminous beings bestowed upon each guardian a sacred artifact, a symbol of their eternal legacy. Dr. Maya Jones received the Celestial Scroll, a mystical tome that contained the collective wisdom of all enlightened beings throughout the ages. With the scroll in her hands, Maya became a custodian of knowledge, entrusted with the task of preserving and disseminating cosmic wisdom to future generations.

Dr. Asvika Bansal was given the Scepter of Unity, a radiant symbol of interconnectedness. With the scepter, Asvika embodied the power to bridge divides, to heal rifts, and to awaken the dormant unity within all beings. She became a guiding light, inspiring harmony and cooperation among the dimensions.

Dr. Arjav Upmanyu received the Cosmic Anvil, a majestic tool forged from the elemental forces themselves. With the anvil, Arjav became a guardian of creation, able to shape and mold the cosmic energies to bring about positive change. He became a steward of balance, ensuring the harmonious coexistence of all beings and elements.

Empowered by their eternal legacy, the gathering of guardians set forth on their final quest—a mission to anchor the energies of cosmic enlightenment into the very core of the multiverse. They traveled to the heart of the Eternal Nexus, where the cosmic energies pulsed with unimaginable power.

In this sacred space, the guardians performed a celestial ritual, channeling their combined cosmic abilities and the wisdom of the luminous beings. They channeled their love, their compassion, and their unwavering commitment to cosmic harmony, infusing the essence of enlightenment into the very fabric of the multiverse.

As the ritual reached its crescendo, a brilliant surge of cosmic energy emanated from the gathering of guardians, rippling through the dimensions. The multiverse responded, resonating with their intention, and cosmic enlightenment spread like a wave, touching every corner of existence.

In the wake of their profound ritual, the gathering of guardians witnessed the transformation of the multiverse. The dimensions shone with a newfound radiance, and beings of all kinds awakened to their true cosmic nature. Love, compassion, and wisdom became the guiding principles, and the pursuit of enlightenment became the cornerstone of existence.

The gathering of guardians realized that their eternal quest had come full circle. They had embarked on a journey of discovery, faced trials and tribulations, delved into the mysteries of the multiverse, and ultimately illuminated the path for others to follow. Their legacy would endure throughout eternity—a testament to their dedication, their courage, and their unwavering belief in the power of cosmic harmony.

With their mission complete, the gathering of guardians returned to the realms they had visited, sharing their wisdom and inspiring others to embark on their own journeys of enlightenment. They became teachers, mentors, and guides, nurturing the seeds of divinity within every sentient being they encountered.

As they spread their cosmic wisdom across the dimensions, the gathering of guardians witnessed the birth of a new era—a golden age of enlightenment and unity. Beings from all corners of existence came together, embracing their cosmic nature and co-creating a harmonious multiverse.

In the final chapter of their saga, the gathering of guardians stood united in the Eternal Nexus, gazing out at the infinite expanse of the multiverse. They basked in the radiance of their eternal legacy, knowing that their work would continue through the eons, carried forward by the hearts and minds of future generations.

Their journey had been one of transformation, discovery, and profound growth. They had transcended the limitations of mortal existence, tapped into the cosmic forces that governed the multiverse, and left an indelible mark on the very essence of creation.

With hearts full of gratitude and spirits ablaze with cosmic light, the gathering of guardians bid farewell to the Eternal Nexus, knowing that their eternal legacy would forever be intertwined with the destiny of the multiverse. They embarked on their own individual paths, guided by the wisdom they had acquired and fueled by the eternal flame of cosmic enlightenment.

And so, the gathering of guardians dispersed across the dimensions, their eternal legacy echoing through the corridors of time. They became beacons of light, illuminating the path for others to follow, inspiring cosmic harmony, and uplifting the consciousness of all sentient beings.

The saga of the gathering of guardians had reached its conclusion, but their cosmic journey continued in the hearts and minds of those they had touched. The multiverse reverberated with their eternal legacy

and the symphony of cosmic harmony they had orchestrated. Their story would be told and retold, inspiring future generations to embark on their own quests for enlightenment and unity.

As the ages unfolded, the multiverse thrived under the guidance of the guardians' eternal legacy. Beings from all corners of existence embraced their cosmic nature, cultivating love, compassion, and wisdom in their interactions with one another. Dimensions once plagued by darkness and discord now shone with the radiance of unity and enlightenment.

The teachings of Dr. Maya Jones, the guardian of wisdom and creativity, spread far and wide. Her celestial melodies resonated in the hearts of seekers, inspiring them to explore the depths of their own knowledge and express their unique gifts. The Celestial Scroll, entrusted to Maya, became a sacred text that guided generations of seekers toward enlightenment and artistic expression.

Dr. Asvika Bansal, the guardian of compassion and empathy, extended her cosmic abilities across the dimensions, healing wounds and fostering understanding. The Scepter of Unity became a symbol of hope and reconciliation, passed down through the generations. Asvika's legacy lived on through the actions of countless beings who embraced compassion as a guiding principle in their lives.

Dr. Arjav Upmanyu, the guardian of harmony and balance, continued to shape the cosmic energies and foster a harmonious relationship between humans and nature. The Cosmic Anvil became a tool of creation, passed down from generation to generation, empowering beings to coexist with the elements and protect the delicate balance of the world. Arjav's legacy endured through the stewardship of the natural world and the pursuit of harmony.

Across the dimensions, enlightened beings emerged, inspired by the eternal legacy of the gathering of guardians. They formed communities of cosmic harmony, centers of wisdom and enlightenment where seekers gathered to learn, grow, and co-create. These centers became beacons of light, radiating the wisdom and compassion that had been passed down through the ages.

As the multiverse continued to evolve, new challenges and opportunities arose. The guardians' eternal legacy guided beings through times of darkness and uncertainty, reminding them of the power of cosmic harmony and the potential within each individual to bring about positive change.

In times of conflict, the teachings of Dr. Maya Jones inspired seekers to seek wisdom and understanding, using their creative abilities to transcend differences and bridge divides. Through art, music, and literature, beings expressed their shared humanity, embracing diversity as a source of strength and unity.

Dr. Asvika Bansal's legacy of compassion guided beings through times of hardship, reminding them to extend a helping hand to those in need. The Scepter of Unity became a symbol of collective responsibility, inspiring acts of kindness and generosity that uplifted communities and fostered a sense of interconnectedness.

Dr. Arjav Upmanyu's teachings on harmony and balance guided beings in their relationship with the natural world. The stewardship of the earth became a collective endeavor, with beings working together to protect and preserve the delicate ecosystems that sustained life across the dimensions. Through sustainable practices and a deep respect for the interconnectedness of all living beings, the legacy of harmony flourished.

As the ages passed, the gathering of guardians became legendary figures, their names etched into the cosmic tapestry of the multiverse. Their eternal legacy continued to shape the destiny of the dimensions, inspiring beings to embrace their cosmic nature and work together towards a harmonious and enlightened existence.

And so, the story of the gathering of guardians came to a close, but their eternal legacy lived on. Their cosmic symphony resonated through the hearts and minds of all beings, guiding them towards unity, compassion, and wisdom. Their journey had been one of transformation, discovery, and growth, leaving an indelible mark on the very essence of creation.

As the multiverse continued to evolve, new guardians would emerge, taking up the mantle and carrying forward the eternal legacy. They would venture into the depths of cosmic mysteries, traverse the dimensions, and weave their own symphony of cosmic harmony.

The eternal legacy of the gathering of guardians would endure, forever entwined with the destiny of the multiverse. And as beings looked to the stars and contemplated the vastness of existence, they would be reminded of the cosmic symphony that echoed through time and space—the symphony that had transformed the dimensions and awakened the dormant spark of divinity within all sentient beings.

And so, the story of the gathering of guardians came to a close, but their eternal legacy lived on. Their cosmic symphony resonated through the hearts and minds of all beings, guiding them towards unity, compassion, and wisdom. Their journey had been one of transformation, discovery, and growth, leaving an indelible mark on the very essence of creation.

As the multiverse continued to evolve, new guardians would emerge, taking up the mantle and carrying forward the eternal legacy. They would venture into the depths of cosmic mysteries, traverse the dimensions, and weave their own symphony of cosmic harmony.

The eternal legacy of the gathering of guardians would endure, forever entwined with the destiny of the multiverse. And as beings looked to the stars and contemplated the vastness of existence, they would be reminded of the cosmic symphony that echoed through time and space—the symphony that had transformed the dimensions and awakened the dormant spark of divinity within all sentient beings.

As the final chapters of their story came to a close, the gathering of guardians stood in awe of the infinite possibilities that lay before them. They knew that their journey had not truly ended, for the cosmic dance of creation would continue to unfold, and new guardians would rise to take their place.

With hearts filled with gratitude and souls ablaze with cosmic light, the gathering of guardians bid farewell to one another, knowing that their paths would cross again in the realms beyond. They ventured forth, guided by the eternal legacy they had forged, ready to embrace new adventures and continue their eternal quest for cosmic harmony and enlightenment.

And so, the gathering of guardians dispersed across the dimensions, their eternal legacy echoing through the corridors of time. They became beacons of light, illuminating the path for others to follow, inspiring cosmic harmony, and uplifting the consciousness of all sentient beings.

The saga of the gathering of guardians had reached its conclusion, but their cosmic journey continued in the hearts and minds of those they had touched. The multiverse reverberated with their eternal legacy, reminding all beings of the power of unity, compassion, and wisdom.

And as the cycles of existence continued to turn, the gathering of guardians would forever be remembered as the harbingers of cosmic harmony

and the guardians of the eternal legacy. Their story would be passed down through the ages, inspiring future generations to embark on their own quests for enlightenment, unity, and cosmic harmony.

Epilogue

As the dust settles and the echoes of their triumph fade away, Dr. Maya Jones and her team find themselves standing on the precipice of a new era. The cataclysm they averted has brought about a profound shift in their understanding of the multiverse and their place within it.

With the cosmic balance restored, Maya, Dr. Asvika Bansal, and Dr. Arjav Upmanyu return to the Institute of Quantum Physics in Mumbai, carrying with them the knowledge and experiences they gained during their extraordinary journey. The once enigmatic discovery of parallel dimensions has now become a cornerstone of their research, leading to groundbreaking advancements in quantum technology and our understanding of the universe.

Their encounters with celestial beings, mythological creatures, and ancient civilizations have left an indelible mark on their souls. Each team member has embraced their unique gifts and abilities, channeling them to benefit humanity and preserve the delicate tapestry of existence.

Beyond their scientific achievements, the team finds solace in the eternal wisdom they have gained. They have come to appreciate the intricate interconnectedness of all things and the profound significance of unity and harmony. Their journey has taught them that true power lies not in dominion but in embracing the interconnected web of life.

As the days turn into years, Dr. Maya Jones, Dr. Asvika Bansal, and Dr. Arjav Upmanyu continue their explorations, delving deeper into the mysteries of the multiverse. Their quest for knowledge has become a lifelong endeavor, one that transcends the boundaries of time and space.

The legacy of their adventures lives on, inspiring generations to come to embrace curiosity, embrace the unknown, and seek the infinite possibilities that lie beyond the veil of reality. The Quantum Mirage, once an enigmatic discovery, now serves as a symbol of human potential and the perpetual quest for understanding.

In the grand tapestry of existence, their story is but one thread, woven intricately into the fabric of time. The multiverse continues to unfold, revealing its secrets to those who dare to venture beyond the confines of what is known. And so, the journey continues, as new horizons beckon and the mysteries of the universe await those who seek to unravel them.

For Dr. Maya Jones and her team, the adventure has only just begun.

And thus, we conclude The Quantum Mirage, a tale that invites us to ponder the wonders of our universe, the power of human curiosity, and the boundless possibilities that lie within our grasp. May it inspire us to embrace the unknown, to question the limits of our understanding, and to embark on our own extraordinary journeys of discovery.

About the Author

Hiren Rathod is an aspiring author and a student pursuing a Bachelor's degree in Computer Engineering. With a passion for writing and storytelling, Hiren has ventured into the realm of fiction to bring imaginative worlds and captivating characters to life. While balancing academic studies, Hiren dedicates time to crafting compelling narratives that blend elements of science fiction, spirituality, and mythology. The Quantum Mirage is Hiren's debut novel, showcasing their creativity and storytelling prowess. As an emerging author, Hiren Rathod is poised to captivate readers with their unique perspective and imaginative storytelling.